PENGUIN BOOKS
Tales of the Tikongs

Epeli Hau'ofa was born in Papua New Guinea in 1938 to
Tongan missionary parents. He went to school in Papua
New Guinea, Tonga, Fiji, and Australia, and attended the
University of New England, Armidale, N.S.W., McGill
University, Montreal, and the Australian National Univer-
sity, Canberra, where he gained a Ph.D in social anthro-
pology. He taught briefly at the University of Papua New
Guinea, and was a research fellow at the University of the
South Pacific in Suva, Fiji. From 1978 to 1981 he was
Deputy Private Secretary to His Majesty the King of
Tonga, and in early 1981 he re-joined the University of the
South Pacific as the first director of the newly created Rural
Development Centre based in Tonga. Since 1983 he has
been Head of the Department of Sociology at the
University.

Epeli Hau'ofa is author of *Kisses in the Nederends*, a novel,
and three works of non-fiction: *Mekeo, Corned Beef and
Tapioca*, and *Our Crowded Islands*. He lives in Suva with his
long-suffering wife Barbara, a stroppy son Epeli Jnr, aged
twelve, and two de-sexed pets, Gipsy and Patch, who pay
him no respect whatsoever.

W9-AFJ-254

Tales of the Tikongs

Epeli Hau'ofa

PENGUIN BOOKS

Penguin Books (N.Z.) Ltd, 182–190 Wairau Road,
Auckland 10, New Zealand
Penguin Books Ltd, Harmondsworth,
Middlesex, England
Penguin Books, 40 West 23rd Street,
New York, N.Y. 10010, U.S.A.
Penguin Books Australia Ltd, Ringwood,
Victoria, Australia
Penguin Books Canada Limited, 2801 John Street,
Markham, Ontario, Canada L3R 1B4

First published by Longman Paul 1983
Published by Penguin Books 1988

Copyright © Epeli Hau'ofa, 1983

All rights reserved

Printed in Hong Kong

To Barbara, Ana, Epeli si'i, Papi, Pusi, and Liklik II

Contents

The Seventh and Other Days

When Jehovah created the Universe in six days and rested on the Seventh, He said it was good and that Man must so regulate his periods of work and rest. The children of Abraham observed the rule, and Christians everywhere do likewise; everywhere, that is, except in the little land of Tiko, notwithstanding its strict Sabbatarian laws. This doesn't mean that Tiko works seven days or even five days a week. No. In order to know its ways of doing things one has to find out first in which direction the Good Lord moves and then think of the opposite of that movement. The Lord moves one way, followed by Christians everywhere, and Tiko goes in the opposite direction, all on its own. Thus if the Lord works six days and rests on the Seventh, Tiko rests six days and works on the Seventh.

'And that's the truth,' said Manu with a firm nod of his heavy head. 'Our people work so hard on Sunday it takes a six-day rest to recover.'

'That's not true!' cried the ancient preacher. 'Nobody works or even plays on Sunday; it's against the law!'

Not wishing to argue with an obstinate octogenarian, Manu told the preacher about his great relative, Sione Falesi.

Sione is a Most Important Person who holds high positions in both the secular and the spiritual affairs of the realm. Sione stands six feet tall, weighs well nigh three hundred pounds, and looks every ounce a great Polynesian aristocrat, as Satusi, his wife of twenty-five years, puts it. Indeed, Sione is a true Polynesian chief, a practising Christian, and a self-confessed sinner who goes to church every Sunday mainly to ask God's forgiveness for his many, many errors.

Sione's house stands not too far from his local church, which has a huge bell. At precisely four-thirty every Sunday morning the big bell booms. Yes, it booms; the bells of Tiko don't peal like those elsewhere. Furthermore the bell at Sione's church booms simultaneously with thousands of other bells throughout the realm, wherein are four times as many churches as all other public establishments combined.

At the first sound of the great boom Sione bounces off his wife and crashes on to the floor stark awake. Satusi also bounces, falls on him, and is very cross because of the interruption. Their sixteen children spring up making nary a noise lest they receive the end of the broom. Everyone in the country jumps up at the same time as Sione and his family. And the bells stop booming only when everyone has gone to church. There is no other way of getting those bells to stop, which explains the almost one hundred per cent church attendance in the realm. Everyone goes to church; everyone, that is, except Manu, who owns the only pair of ear-plugs in the country. And Manu stays fast asleep.

That's how Sunday begins in tiny Tiko; and there is a long day ahead. Every two hours the big bells boom, and every two hours everyone but Manu goes to church. Everyone prays, everyone sings, everyone confesses; on their seats, on their feet, and on their knees. And thoughout the Seventh Day the Lord is praised, the Lord is flattered, and the Lord is begged. Though perhaps the Lord doesn't hear if it's His day off.

The final act of piety takes place at 10.00 p.m. when each family gathers to say the family prayer before it retires to a well-earned six-day rest and recovery period.

Sione has sixteen children, none of whom was born on a Sunday. His wife is pregnant again and it is absolutely certain that the child will enter this world on any day but the Seventh. Indeed no one in the realm has ever been conceived or born from sunrise to midnight on a Sunday, on account of the bells which keep people inside the churches. It's impossible to commit sin of any kind on the Seventh Day. Babies could be born on Sundays, say the doctors at the National Hospital, only if their makers had sinned on this day. But no one does, not even Sione, although he is a Most Important Person.

'The Seventh is the Day of the Lord; every other day belongs to Satan,' Manu explained. And Satan, as Teachers of Sunday School say, does nothing but lead people into Temptation. Thus the six days that belong to Satan are not only a period of rest and recovery, but also of Temptation and much, much sin.

Yet notwithstanding their pious demeanour and assertions to the contrary, Sione and his friends would have it no other way. So through rest and oh such awful sin during the six days after the Seventh, Sione has sired sixteen children, with more yet to come. Sione firmly believes that by raising a large family he is doing the Almighty a handsome favour. Didn't Jehovah tell Abraham to produce as many issue as there are grains of sand on earth or stars in the firmament? Yes, Jehovah did, said Sione, and there aren't yet as many people in Tiko as there are grains in even a handful of sand.

So Sione inevitably opposes the Family Planning Association (FPA) and what it represents. When the Association talked of the population explosion, Sione retorted that there aren't any explosions in Tiko except from behinds of members of the FPA. When the Association reasoned that if people rest less they will procreate less, Sione countered that rest and procreation are God's gifts to Man and have, therefore, nothing to do with the FPA. When the Association appealed to the clergy to lighten the Sunday burden so that people would not spend so much time resting at home on other days, the clergy would not countenance the suggestion, proclaiming that only when their flocks go to Heaven will they rest on a Sunday. Their flocks, said the clergy, may rest as much as they want on other days. And rest they do: at home, in the bush, on chairs, everywhere.

Sione, for example, drives every morning from Monday to Friday to his office to loaf on the chair behind his desk. At three o'clock every day from Monday to Friday he hurries home to spend the rest of the day on his wife.

None of this does any good whatever for National Development, said the Wise Men at the Thinking Office. These

Men of Wisdom once hired an Overseas Expert to look into the feasibility of making Tikongs work on weekdays.

The expert, a certain Mr Merv Dolittle from the Department of Aboriginal Affairs, Canberra, Australia, interviewed half a dozen Very Important Persons, the last being Sione Falesi. Mr Dolittle arrived at Sione's office an hour earlier than had been arranged and found him playing cards with his secretary, Ana Taipe.

'Well, come in, come in, Mr Dolittle. You're rather early aren't you?' Sione greeted his guest with no sign of embarrassment. 'Would you like to play five hundred with us? No? What a pity. Take a seat, then. We're just having our morning-tea break.'

'Morning-tea break?' queried Mr Dolittle, glancing at his watch. It was nine o'clock. His eyes scanned the office for teacups.

'You won't see anything, Mr Dolittle. We have no money for tea so we kill the allotted time playing cards. If you can't feed your face you may as well fiddle with your fingers. That's what I always say. Ana, clear the desk and take the cards with you. Good girl. We'll resume at lunch-time.'

The secretary left the office and Sione turned to the expert. 'Nice girl that one. She's the sharpest card player in Tiko. That's why I hired her. She's not much good at anything else though. All our good ones are in New Zealand.'

'What does Ana do?'

'All sorts of things, Mr Dolittle. She and I play cards at morning-tea time and at lunch-time. Every so often we get into the spirit of things and play on. What's two hours here and there, I ask you?'

'What else does she do?'

'All sorts of things, like I said,' said Sione, racking his brain for Ana's positive attributes. 'She's a damn good masseuse. I've got this slipped disc you see, and she's been fixing it for five years now. Every day, in fact. She's tremendous; you must try her sometime.'

'Is your work-load heavy, Mr Falesi?'

'Oh yes, very heavy indeed. You should see me on Sundays when I work eighteen hours non-stop for God. Life's a burden, an enormous burden,' said Sione, sighing heavily. 'But one must do one's bit for the Almighty. He's been very good to Tiko; you can see it all around. . . .'

'What about the other days?' Mr Dolittle cut in.

'What? Oh, yes. The other days, of course. Well, you see, Mr Dolittle. . . .' Sione stopped as if something had suddenly struck him. Then a wide grin creased his face. 'Incredible!' he ejaculated. 'How about that?'

'How about what?'

'Your name. Dolittle. It's so beautiful! Heavens above, you must be one of us! Ana! Ana! Bring the cards back in!'

'I must say that I've never, in all my life...' Mr Dolittle began to protest, then thought better of it, rose, excused himself, and beat a hasty exit. The incident was more than sufficient to enable him to grasp the nature of the problem. He wound up his tour that very day, called a press conference, and declared that this lot of natives, like the Aborigines, had an enormous untapped potential for work; but that His Excellency's Government must first import the Protestant Ethic, two little words hitherto unheard of in the realm, although most Tikongs are Protestants. When Radio AP2U broadcast and explained the full meaning of the said ethic, the entire population suddenly turned deaf.

'And deafness comes from too much rest,' Manu proclaimed.

When one rests too much one grows too many hairs inside one's ears, blocking out all sounds except the voice of flattery. That's why people of the common order, the vast majority of Tikongs, are the most adept flatterers in the Pacific: they have spent so much time practising it. And to many Important Persons, the so-called Sitters-on-Chairs, Wise Men, Traumatised Experts, Devious Traders, and assorted Pulpit Poops, flattery is sweeter than ice cream.

One of these Sitters-on-Chairs is, of course, Manu's gigantic relative Sione, nemesis of the Family Planning Association and father of sixteen children. One Monday morning Sione was sitting behind the desk of his office. The desk top was shining clean with nothing on it except a copy of *Penthouse* magazine confiscated from a visiting American yacht.

5

Sione's foreign-aid adviser, to whom he has delegated all his work, entered the office on this lovely Monday morning to announce that their agency was on the verge of bankruptcy. Sione sat motionless staring through the window; not a muscle moved. He heard nothing, he saw nothing; he was in deep repose as always on the first day after the Seventh.

The foreign-aid adviser nevertheless perceived that as soon as he opened his mouth the three-inch hairs protruding from Sione's ears began to bunch up, blocking the ear-holes as effectively as Manu's ear-plugs. The adviser mumbled a profanity, stalked out in disgust, and lost his way, eventually finding himself, as usual, slumped over the bar of the Tiko Club.

Immediately afterwards the underpaid agency cleaner, Lea Fakahekeheke, crept into the office, insinuated himself behind Sione, and whispered thus into his ear: 'Most Respected Sir, the New Zealand Aid Delegation which came last Friday told me you're the wisest and most handsome man in the whole world.'

Even before Lea moved his lips the hairs in Sione's ears, as if anticipating what was coming, disentagled themselves and conducted the honeyed words swiftly into his brain. He suddenly came alive, breaking into a smile, yelling and hugging Lea.

Then he unlocked the agency safe, pulled out two five-dollar bills, and pressed them into Lea's half-unwilling hands, ordering him to take the day off. Lea slithered away well satisfied.

Every second week for over fifteen years Lea has gone to the office to whisper nice things into Sione's ear, and the Great Man has never failed to reward him each time with no less than ten dollars, which is considerably more than his fortnightly earnings.

'And who leads whom in Tiko?' Manu asked, never for a moment expecting a reply.

The Winding Road to Heaven

'Religion and Education Destroy Original Wisdom' cry the letters on the back of Manu's shirt. 'Over Influenced' says the front of the same garment. The wearer of the said shirt is one of the best known characters in Tiko; and although His Excellency is the most famous, Manu runs a very close second. As for telling it like it is, Manu is the only teller of big truths in the realm. This is not to suggest that our country comprises a nation of liars as some uninitiated foreigners seem to think, far from it. Truth comes in portions, some large, some small, but never whole. Like our ancestors we are expert tellers of half-truths, quarter-truths, and one-percent truths. When Tevita Alanoa stole his neighbour's pig and protested, after being caught, that he had only eaten one leg, he was telling a quarter-truth. And when he affirmed that his victimised neighbour was his mother's brother and that therefore he, Tevita, was not really a thief, he was telling a half-truth. And furthermore, when he got carried away and said that his mother's brother's pigs were for him to take without asking, and was punched on the nose by his uncle, Tevita was telling a one-percent truth.

You can get away nicely with half-truths and quarter-truths, and indeed most people do so with joyful frequency; but it is not so easy to escape unscathed with one-percent truths, as Tevita discovered with a bloodied nose. Even the act of telling a one-percent truth requires a good measure of sophistication, acquired only after having completed six years of Modern Education at a church college. Consider the case of Inoke Nimavave who forged and cashed a cheque for $100.

When hauled into court Inoke argued, after he had sworn on the Bible, that it was all the fault of the cross-eyed cashier at the Bank of Tiko. According to the defence the defective clerk had misread the cheque as $100 instead of the correct $1.00, the small amount Inoke needed for his taxi fare to the hospital to visit his dying mother. And why did he not return the ninety-nine point zero zero dollars to the cross-eyed clerk at the Bank of Tiko? asked the police magistrate. Inoke wept and replied with a question so phrased that it tore the heart of everyone in the courtroom on that warm, warm October morning. How, he appealed, could he think of money when all the thoughts in his head were with his poor mum who was on her way to Heaven? How could he indeed; and the angels wept, and the police magistrate wept and gave Inoke a six-month sentence with hard labour. Poor Inoke; his fellow inmates called him Zero Zero, which was most misleading since he was a brilliant arithmetician and a top graduate of Potopoto College.

If telling a one-percent truth is difficult, telling less than a one-percent truth is telling lies, which is almost impossible. That is why there are so very few liars in Tiko; they can be smelled out quickly, and everyone calls them 'loi'elo' which means 'stinking liars'. And as our people hate a bad smell, especially when it emanates from the mouth, they rarely tell lies.

Those who believe that truth, like beauty, is straight and narrow should not visit our country or they will be led up the garden path or sold down the river (so to speak, since we have no rivers). Truth is flexible and can be bent this way so and that way so; it can be stood on its head, be hidden in a box, and be sat upon. Only Manu treads the straight and narrow path, followed by no one because that path exists entirely in his head. Most real roads on our islands are very narrow, very crooked, and full of pot holes. Here no second-hand bus from Suva lasts more than six months. There are a few straight roads with no pot holes, but they are all in the bush where they serve no good purpose. The Good Book says the honest man walks that straight and narrow path, but alas! our straight roads are much too wide; and that is why they are used mainly by thieves helping themselves to their neighbours' gardens.

All pathways outside Manu's head go against the injunction of the Good Book: they are straight and wide or narrow and crooked. And walking spaces in government buildings are even more perilous for an honest man: there are no paths in those offices. Civil servants negotiate their way between untidy desks and often bump into Temptation from which no one could be delivered by the Lord's Prayer. After lunch one afternoon Semisi Nokutu returned to his departmental office before anyone else. He was a typical civil servant: semi-honest and half-trusted. As he snaked his way among the untidy desks and filing cabinets on this fine, fine afternoon Semisi bumped into something from which a large brown envelope fell on to the floor before his eyes. He picked up the envelope, opened it, found $200 and, being a half-honest civil servant, put back $100. After work he went home, set aside $50 for his annual missionary contribution, asked God's forgiveness, spent $25 on beer for himself, and the rest on filmy pink panties for his Suva-style ladyfriend. Semisi always did everything by halves. And no one besides himself and the Good Lord would have known of the incident had it not been for a most unfortunate occurrence. On the eve of his retirement, twenty-five years after the aforementioned event, Semisi had a stroke which paralysed his left side from head to toe. He also went half-mad and confessed all his sins publicly, including the desk-and-envelope incident. This did him little good, for his other side succumbed to paralysis and he died; the preacher at his funeral proclaimed that Semisi had been forgiven by the Lord and had gone to Heaven.

'And lead us not into Temptation...', but businessmen bump into it so often nobody believes there is such a thing as an honest man of means. Ofa Kākā, ex-owner of the biggest fleet of motorised tricycles in Tulisi and owner of the most prosperous peanut-selling venture in the whole of Tiko, was the treasurer of the Trustees' Committee of his local church. Some years ago his church gathered $20 000 in its annual Missionary Collection, most of the money coming from harassed and persecuted overstayers in New Zealand.

On the morning after the collection Ofa took off on an aeroplane to Pagopago; he also took a briefcase filled with $20 000, and the last heard of him was that he had gone to California disguised as an American Samoan.

And, as Manu says, not even the clergy are safe from Temptation. These holy men live in villages with paths so narrow, crooked, and slippery that only one villager at a time can walk safely on them. If on a dark and moonless night two people walk on the same path from opposite directions there is bound to be an accident or something worse. On one such dark and moonless night two travellers of opposite sex walked on the same path from opposite directions. One was the local clergyman. The nocturnal walkers inevitably collided, and on the following day the clergyman was expelled on the grounds of his having committed an unchristian act on the person of a parishioner. A band of dirty little boys, returning from a raid on someone's mango tree, had witnessed the awful act. The ex-holy man banished himself to a church farm on another island where he spent a brief period praying for forgiveness so he might still go to Heaven.

'And forgive us our trespasses as we forgive those who trespass against us . . . .' Forgiveness pours down fast and generously like rain in March. It is the Christian virtue most ardently sought and most freely bestowed in the realm. God forgives your sins no matter what they are, if you ask Him. And you must forgive others, always. So everyone forgives everything all the time; and everyone forgives things to come and things that have passed. And only yesterday I forgave Faihala's great-great-grandfather's sins against my great-great-grandmother. And not so long ago, when five very, very important men discovered that they had together helped themselves to half a million dollars of public money to which they had no right to help themselves, they prayed for God's forgiveness, they forgave each other, and they neither had to resign from their very important jobs nor return any money to anyone.

'Thine be the Glory!' cry the letters on the back of Manu's shirt.

Old Wine in New Bottles

Manu's distant relative, Hiti George VI, has a bicycle—an ancient affair by Tikong or by any other standards. The machine is a genuine mid-1940s BSA bought by Hiti's father at a time when the good citizens of Birmingham, England, were still a proud, honest folk who built strong, everlasting bicycles each of which could, and did, carry a Tikong family of four: dad, mum, and two little ones. Dad pedalled the cycle, mum sat sideways on the cross-bar, the littlest one perched on the handle-bar, held by his mother, and the less little one stood near the rear-wheel axle holding on to his father's back. In this way the family went to church, visited relatives, or pedalled anywhere they cared to go. Those were the days when there were only a few motor-vehicles in Tiko, when most families had push-bikes, and when the workers of Birmingham, England, were makers of strong, everlasting BSAs.

Hiti was born in 1939, a few months before the King of England called battle on the Fuehrer of Germany on account of the latter's beastliness toward his neighbours. On the occasion of the child's birth, his father, a descendant of a proud nineteenth-century Bavarian trader and a high-ranking local lady of doubtful propriety, called him Hitler. But when the King declared war on the Fuehrer, the father quickly changed his son's name by crossing out the last three letters and adding an extra 'i', on account of Tiko being part of the Great British Empire, but more so because of the Tikong government's grabbing Bavarian descendants who showed any sign of pride in the Fuehrer and putting them behind bars as suspected enemy agents. The father went further and added

'George VI' to his son's new name, thereby declaring his allegiance to the King of England and to His Excellency the Paramount Chief of Tiko and Great Friend of England and Empire.

Hiti loves old things, especially his old BSA. He literally grew up on the English bicycle his father bought in 1945 to commemorate the Victory over the Fuehrer. The family of four went everywhere on that machine. At first little Hiti perched on the handle-bar; then, as he grew taller, graduated to standing at the back holding on to his father's generous midriff. When, at the age of nine, he learnt how to ride bicycles, his dad, a semi-honest man of means, bought a new BSA and gave the old one to Hiti. Hiti has kept that ancient machine to this very day, treating it with tender care. Whenever he is worried or distressed he hops on his bicycle and pedals all over Tulisi and even the surrounding villages until he regains tranquillity.

The bicycle is one of the innumerable old things with which Hiti surrounds himself. Like ninety-nine per cent of his countrymen Hiti likes to make new things look very old very quickly before he can love them dearly. For instance, besides his old bicycle Hiti has a small Toyota sedan which he bought brand-new eighteen months ago for the transportation of his family of nine, not counting assorted uncles, aunts, nephews, and nieces. When he acquired the vehicle, so made as to carry no more than four short, slight Japanese, Hiti promptly filled it with six hefty Tikongs. In a matter of months the Tikongs grew large while the Toyota shrank. Both rear-view mirrors and the hub-caps have disappeared, and most of the paint has gone. The seats are torn, a side window is smashed, and the engine is tied and patched with chicken-wire and Band-Aids. The car looks very old and very sick, and Hiti loves it dearly. He takes good care of it now, and the Toyota sedan, like other motor-vehicles in Tiko, will sputter on for the next fifteen years although its makers had intended it to last no more than seven.

Hiti also loves people—after he has aged them properly that is. Two examples will illustrate this point. On turning twenty, Hiti began leading a dissolute life although he had graduated as the top student of his school in matters scholastic, moral, and spiritual. Every year as a student Hiti took the three most important prizes: first in the class, first in goodness, and first in Scriptural knowledge. Upon his graduation, his father, mother, and entire extended family thought that he would eventually become a Cabinet Minister or the President of the Sabbatarian Church. Hiti became neither and has nary a chance of becoming either. When, at twenty, he saw the pleasure in things neither so good nor so pure, Hiti began tasting forbidden fruits and sowing wild seeds. He tasted and sowed so much that within five years he had sired nine lovely children by seven former virgins. He stopped going to church, became an alcoholic, and abused his parents. He was defrocked as a preacher, expelled from his lucrative job, and sent thrice to gaol for disorderly behaviour.

Shamed and distressed, his parents aged overnight; a nervous breakdown drove his mother to senility at forty-eight, and a heart condition hastened his father's decline. One day, when accidentally sober, Hiti looked at his withering parents and his old BSA and sobbed and sobbed with remorse. A week later he became an Evangelical, discarded his sinful ways along with any sign of individuality, cut his hair, and wore very clean clothes and a short, shiny tie. Soon after, he spent three years as a missionary beating the streets of Tulisi converting dissolute Sabbatarians. His parents recovered their health somewhat, but remained prematurely old; and Hiti loves them most dearly.

Through family connections and old school ties Hiti regained his former job, but his alcoholic past had wreaked such havoc with his brain that he was totally incompetent and was therefore promoted to a higher post in which most of his work was done by an adviser from Abingdon, England. Mr Charlès Edward George Higginbotham was a tall, thin, round-shouldered man of thirty-five who looked not a day older than sixty, and Hiti, who made him aged and wise in quick-time, loved him dearly.

Mr Higginbotham was the son of a powerful knight who, using family connections and old school ties, entered Charles Edward into the civil service hoping that he would one day become the permanent head of a major department. Young Charles also had the same idea and worked most diligently. But his ambition was so naked that his threatened superiors conspired to send him as far away from London as possible, even to the end of the world. Thus when an advisory position in a remote needy country was advertised they commended him with enthusiam. He readily accepted the five-year secondment not because of any love for sunshine, but because he was to be paid by the International Aid Distribution Agency with a tax-free annual salary of $30 000, which was seven times more than he was earning as a servant of the Queen of England.

The generous remuneration included allowances for living away from the sweetness of home, for being deprived of the civilising influence of television, for the inconvenience of having to live with cockroaches, rats, and scrawny dogs, for the exposure of refined, sensitive skin to mosquitoes, bugs, and sandflies, for risking contraction of such foreign diseases as cholera, typhoid, and the clap and, finally, for the danger of being mauled by insatiable native nymphomaniacs.

Upon his arrival in Tiko Mr Higginbotham was assigned to advise Hiti George VI. Charles Edward soon discovered that his code of civil service ethics was totally opposed to that of Hiti. During the second week of work he suspected that just about everyone who worked in the office was an uncle, a cousin, a nephew, or a niece of Hiti's.

'I say, is everyone here related to you?'

'We're one big, happy family, yes.'

'Isn't that rather odd?'

Hiti was taken aback. 'You're not being critical of our family system, are you?'

'Absolutely not. I wouldn't dream of it. Nevertheless, one shouldn't recruit one's relatives to public jobs. It's not quite ethical, I should say,' said Charles Edward, forgetting how he had got his London job.

'What's unethical about helping your relatives and friends? Look at the other offices. Look at the Churches. They're all big happy families.'

'I see,' said Charles Edward trying to hide his amazement.

'I wonder,' he ventured after a while, 'I wonder what will happen to the Service and the Churches if families are none too bright?'

'Other families ARE none too bright!' Hiti shot back, dismissing the subject.

Charles Edward was dumbfounded. He wanted to say more but was mindful of the $30 000 salary which he had no wish to jeopardise. He went home very disturbed and on that night developed a nasty and persistent case of migraine. Thus began Charles Edward's decline.

A few days later he arrived at the office to find Hiti and no one else.

'I say, where is everyone?'

'At the feast.'

'What feast, may I ask?'

'A family feast.'

'Do you mean to say that everyone's gone to a family feast during working hours?'

Hiti pretended not to hear. Charles Edward looked outside at the empty parking lot. 'I suppose the departmental vehicles have also gone to the feast?'

'That's right.'

'Why, for Heaven's sake?'

'To transport the workers to and fro.'

Charles Edward couldn't believe his ears. 'But departmental vehicles have nothing to do with private family affairs.'

Hiti merely stared, giving him the silent treatment Tikongs have long found most effective in dealing with nosy foreigners. Speechless, impotent, and utterly indignant, Charles Edward stalked out, went home, and drank a full bottle of whisky. He drank heavily the following day and the day after and soon became addicted. Events to which he was morally unaccustomed piled up, each taking a heavy toll on Charles Edward's physical and mental health. By the end of his first year of service he was already a sick old man, and Hiti began to love him dearly.

Hiti saw to it that Charles Edward was undisturbed and comfortable by giving him practically nothing to do. Anything controversial or questionable, which was just about everything, bypassed his desk. And Hiti recruited a Peace Corps volunteer to carry most of the burden.

On Charles Edward's final day in Tiko, Hiti gave him a farewell feast. It started at ten in the morning with a two-hour thanksgiving prayer by a certain clergyman, followed by four hours of speeches by Hiti and every relative working in his office. The feast concluded at five in the evening with a one-hour closing prayer conducted again by the aforementioned Man of the Cloth.

That night Charles Edward feared he had developed piles from sitting too long on damp ground during the feast. He also had food-poisoning and acute diarrhoea from eating cold chicken and roast pork. On the following morning all the workers went to say farewell to their adviser, who looked so ill, so miserable, and so old that everyone, most of all Hiti, wept copiously as they waved goodbye. It was the most moving send-off ever staged at the Tikomalu International Airport. Charles Edward George Higginbotham, old man at forty and beloved of Hiti George VI, died midway between Tiko and Auckland on Flight BG320.

Meanwhile Hiti had returned from the airport to his office to deal with the Peace Corps volunteer, who has turned out to be a hopeless case. Young, and a long-standing dropout from his growth-crazed society, the volunteer resolutely refuses to be affected by anything happening around him. No one loves him for he remains obstinately youthful despite everything. Being raised among the slippery Polynesian emigrants in Oakland, California, the volunteer deciphers the South Sea code, and has roundly beaten his fellow-workers at their own games. If they put the departmental vehicles to personal use once a day, he does it twice; if they go on sick leave twice a fortnight, he goes four times, spending much of it drinking beer and playing snooker at the Tiko Club. When, at private parties to which no ordinary Tikongs are invited, some foreign advisers, oozing rectitude, decry the rampant corruption and nepotism in the realm, the Peace Corps volunteer merely shrugs his shoulders saying, 'So, what else is new in the world?' And Hiti, who cannot drive him into self-righteousness and hence into early old age, despises him most heartily.

Not being able to deal with the smart American, Hiti has taken to riding his old BSA all over Tulisi and the neighbouring villages, taking consolation in the very sight of shabbiness and decrepitude surrounding him. The newly patched roads along which he pedals are so full of dust and pot holes they make nonsense of the thirty-mile-an-hour speed limit imposed throughout the island: nothing crawls faster than twenty miles an hour on those roads unless it be a new vehicle its owner wants to age in a hurry. Most houses along Hiti's cycling routes, recently built with money earned by temporary migrant labourers in New Zealand, have gathered layers of dust and mould and have assumed a look of deep antiquity. Others lean on long bamboo poles as support against gentle breezes. And Hiti loves them all: the roads, the houses, the scrawny dogs, the aged young, the healthy, grubby children, everyone and everything he sees from his bicycle, except...except those plots of land in each settlement covered with mounds of gleaming sand. Those quiet acres of sandy knolls, the cleanest, whitest, freshest, and only well-maintained things in the whole country, are the shiny cemeteries of Tiko.

'God bless the Whited Sepulchres!' Manu cried as he pedalled past Hiti on his brand-new Hercules.

The Tower of Babel

'Tiko can't be developed,' Manu declared, 'unless the ancient gods are killed.'

'But the ancient gods are dead. The Sabbatarians killed them long ago,' countered the ancient preacher.

'Never believe that, sir. Had they died Tiko would have developed long ago. Look around you,' Manu advised.

The ancient preacher looked around and saw nothing; he looked at himself, his tattered clothes, his nailed-in second-hand sandals, and nodded rather dubiously. He wished to be developed. 'And how do you slay the ancient gods?' he inquired cautiously.

'Never try, sir, it's useless,' Manu replied. 'Kill the new ones.' And that, in short, is what Manu does. He wants to keep the ancient gods alive and slay the new ones. He pedals his bicycle to the International Nightlight Hotel, to the Bank of Tiko, and all over Tulisi, shouting his lonely message against Development, but the whole capital is as a cemetery.

And Manu shouted at the Doctor of Philosophy recently graduated from Australia. The good Doctor works on Research for Development. He is a portly man going to pot a mite too soon for his age; and he looks an oddity with an ever-present pipe protruding from his bushy, beefy face. The Doctor is an Expert, although he has never discovered what he is an expert of. It doesn't matter; in the balmy isles of Tiko, as long as one is Most Educated, one is Elite, an Expert, and a Wise Man to boot.

One starry evening the portly Doctor walked down a dusty Tulisi street. He walked the walk of those who would build Tiko higher than the Tower of Babel. The good Doctor walked loftily. Then out of the blue, on this clear and starry night, a piercing voice sliced the stillness with, 'WHY ARE YOU DESTROYING MY COUNTRY?' It was Manu, who knows how to pierce.

Manu also shouted at the Great Secretary, a young man with an enormous mop on his head. The Secretary is a Most Important Person, an Expert, Elite, and a Wise Man to boot. This happy combination of four great elements in the person of one so young has turned the Secretary into a Man of Substance with a bright and prosperous future in the development of his country.

One sunny day he was driving through the main street of downtown Tulisi, waving to all and sundry, who waved back, impressed with his Friendliness and Humility. With Wise Men like him, say all and sundry, the development of the realm is in Good Hands. The Secretary was driving to the Bank of Tiko to draw $50 000 for the funding of a Great Development Project. He was very pleased with himself. Then suddenly a slashing voice split the steamy asphalt: 'TIKO HATES YOU!' The Secretary was so surprised he ran his automobile into an old raintree outside the Bank of Tiko. The voice was Manu's, and Manu knows how to drive a man up a tree.

Tiko can't be developed, said Manu with the certainty of someone who knows. But the Wise Men of Tiko want to develop everything; everything, that is, except sex. Sex is too developed already; why else would Tiko have the highest population growth rate in the Pacific? Furthermore, was not sex responsible for the Fish Cannery Project fiasco?

The great cannery project revolved around the fishing vessel, the *Maumau Taimi*, which originated in Japan and had a refrigerated compartment to hold one hundred tons of tuna. In Japanese hands it operated well around the Pacific waters for twenty years before the owners decided that instead of converting it into scrap metal they would send it to Tiko as aid to needy foreign friends.

The *Hata Maru*, as it was known in Tokyo, was crewed by Japanese men none of whom was younger than sixty-five. The elderly hands, whose sex drive had long gone dry, as they say around the dockyards of the Orient, would go out for three or four months until the one-hundred-ton hold was filled to the hatch with tuna.

When the Japanese envoy presented the vessel at Tulisi to His Excellency's Government he did not reveal this clever operating method, because the Japanese, whose country is managed by a gerontocracy, did not wish to let it be known that their old men are of little value to women. They did not want to lose face.

The vessel's arrival created high expectations that Tiko would shortly become a Nation with a Fish Cannery. The *Maumau Taimi* has been around for ten years now, but there is still not a cannery. The vessel could have long ago been passed on to New Zealand as a foreign-aid item, but the Wise Men at the Thinking Office do not want to lose face.

And what's behind this failure? 'Sex!' said Manu without hesitation. And he is right. The vessel's arrival coincided with a period of much anxiety concerning the too many young men walking the streets of Tulisi; doing nothing, according to high officialdom. In actual fact the young men had been doing many, many things, like looking for a bit of sex most of the time; but the Appropriate Authorities did not let this be known, for fear of losing face. And the Appropriate Authorities persuaded the young men to crew the newly acquired vessel as a way of doing something and as part of their contribution to the development of Tiko.

The first of their projected ninety days at sea was very nice, and the next few days at sea were also very nice. But by the end of the second week the much deprived youths wanted desperately to set for home and a bit of sex. On the third week nothing would keep them away and the vessel headed home with only four tons of tuna. The operating costs for the trip ran close to $8000 and the sale of the catch brought in not quite $2000. It's been that way since the *Maumau Taimi* ventured forth on its Tikong maiden voyage. No one says anything, no one does anything, for no one dares lose face.

In developing the realm into a Nation with a Fish Cannery it was necessary to develop not only the Top but also the

Bottom, in order to get a proper balance. 'A well-rounded Bottom below a well-rounded Top is beauty well worth having,' Manu declared, not thinking of tinned fish.

The responsibility for Bottom Development went to one Alvin (Sharky) Lowe of Alice Springs, Australia. Mr Lowe, a matey-matey sort of bloke who wanted to be known simply as Sharky, was a Great Expert with lifelong experience in handling natives in New Guinea, Thursday Island, and in a certain humpy settlement outside his gentle hometown of Alice Springs. He had developed a good feel for the Grass-roots, demonstrating it by grabbing every frightened, small-time, part-time fisherman on the beaches of Tulisi and forcing him ever so gently to accept $4000 in Development Loans from the Appropriate Authorities. And, like the Great Shepherd of Nazareth, Sharky converted many frightened fellows into fishermen.

One such frightened, small-time, part-time fisherman was Ika Levu, who happened also to be a small-time, part-time gardener. His dual occupation meant that Ika worked whenever he felt like it; and he had very little money, which bothered him not at all. Ika never felt miserable until Sharky laid hands on him. It was his most urgent duty to help develop his country, said Sharky.

Mr Lowe had originally found him on a beach one day caulking a leaky old dinghy. 'Hello there. I'm Sharky, and I'm the Fisheries Grassroots Development Adviser. Do you speak English?'

'Eh, a leetol bit.'

'You no can speak English good?' Sharky switched to the language he used when talking to simple natives.

'Eh, a leetol bit.'

'Whassat name belong you?'

'Eh, a leetol bit.'

'Leetol bit? You no leetol bit! You beeg fela bit! Look, me try one more time yet.' Sharky took a deep breath, then resumed speaking, very slowly and very clearly this time. 'Now, me like savvy name belong you. All right? Name belong you Joe? or Jack? or....'

'Oi, me Ika Levu.'

'Good fela name, Ika. Me like it too much. You go catch fish sometime?'

'Eh, a leetol bit.'

'Good, good. Now suppose you help me develop country belong you, me help you catch plenty big fela fish. You savvy?'

Ika didn't quite get it so he shrugged and turned away. Sharky grabbed his shoulders, turned him around, and put all his salemanship into operation. 'Now is duty belong you to help Tiko come up rich fela country. Suppose you help Tiko, me help you too. Like me help you get one big fela loan, na you can buy new boat, na fishing nets, na lines, na hooks, na floats. Plenty something you can buy. Then you go catch big fela fish, na you sell em, na you get plenty money, na you can buy six fela Marys inside International Nightlight Hotel, pushpush no stop all time good! Me think think you clever fela man. You strong up there, you strong down below like four fela Brahmin bullmacow. Now you me work allgather onetime like brothers. Me big brother, you little brother. You me help Tiko come up all same big fela rich country. Plenty plenty ice cream, sweet sweet all same lollies from Heaven. All right?'

'Me doan know.'

'You no can savvy? Gawd! Me talk talk all same simple something na you no can savvy! Whassamatter? Me think think head belong you too much dumdum na full up shit something no good true! All right, me all same try one more time yet, na you try savvy good or I'll bloody well bash your coon head in, O.K.?'

So with the infinite patience and gentleness of an expert native handler Sharky went through the whole routine a few more times until Ika got the message. Ika was thoroughly frightened and confused. He was also flattered. No Important Person had ever before sought his help, let alone talked to him. And although he was full of doubt Ika prayed to God for guidance and consented to accept the loan.

With Sharky's help Ika acquired a twelve horse-power Rendo outboard motor, an eighteen-foot imported dinghy, six big nets, and dozens of lines and hooks, all of which came from certain firms in Japan and Australia which Sharky represented.

When Ika was properly equipped and properly launched for a lifetime of catching the big fish, Sharky moved on to the next fisherman, and to the next. By the time his tour of duty ended Sharky had equipped and launched one thousand fishermen with one thousand Rendo outboard motors, one thousand imported dinghies, six thousand big nets, and tens of thousands of lines and hooks. Sharky had also established a Fishermen's Aid Post furnished with spare parts and a stock of Rendo motors, imported dinghies, and big nets, all of which came from those certain companies in Japan and Australia of which he was the sole South Pacific Representative. In helping the development of Tiko, Sharky had helped the development of himself and his companies most generously.

And what of Ika, the frightened little man embarked on his solemn duty toward the development of his country? As soon as he got his fishing equipment, and got himself thoroughly in debt, Sharky dropped him and forgot about his existence. No one thought of guiding him, so he remained a small-timer and part-timer in everything. Like other such fishermen Ika never met the Appropriate Authorities: they simply could not be seen.

The first time Ika tried to see them he was so nervous that he stood outside the office door for twenty minutes before he could summon sufficient courage to knock; and his knock was so gentle that it hardly made a sound. Another twenty minutes went by before he mustered enough courage to open the door ever so slightly and peek in. A plumpish receptionist was sitting at a desk only ten feet away, talking to a fellow-worker. Ika coughed a bit to attract their attention.

'What do you want?' asked the receptionist, obviously annoyed with the interruption. She had just resumed duty that morning after two-months' maternity leave.

'Please miss. I want to talk to someone....'

'He's not here. Come back tomorrow.'

'Forgive me, miss, I think it's important. It's about the payments of a loan I got from this office.'

'Well, come right in then; I won't eat you. Do you have

the instalment on you?'

'That's what I want to talk to someone about. You see, I haven't got anything with me.'

'I see. You'd better discuss that with the Assistant Secretary. Mele!' she called out to someone in the main office behind her, 'is the A.S. in?'

'No. He's gone to Wellington to attend a conference. He'll be back in two weeks.'

'How about the Director then?'

'He's gone with the Minister to Geneva. They'll be back next month after meetings in Rome, Tel Aviv, New Delhi, Djakarta, and Sydney. Lucky pigs; their pockets won't be big enough to hold their travel allowances. Why can't they send us sometime for a change?'

'And Dau Yali?'

'That idiot is in London on a six-month training course. He has no brains, but he's the Director's cousin. They're all overseas, the whole bloody lot of them.'

'But who's holding the fort?'

'Who do you think but the likes of us?'

The receptionist turned to Ika. 'Well, you heard what the situation is. Go home and come back in a month's time. Don't look so depressed, for goodness' sake. It's nothing new. Look, I'll try the crowd downstairs. They may be able to help you.'

She picked up the telephone and dialled a number. 'Seini? Susana. Very well thanks; and you? That's good, but don't overdo it. Look, is Vakarau Dro in?'

'No,' came the voice from the other end, 'he's in bed with gout and won't be in for the rest of the week.'

'But he'll be back next week, won't he?'

'Sort of. He'll come in to pick up his papers and then he's off straightaway to a seminar in Kuala Lumpur. From there he goes to Tokyo to represent the Ministry at the Tayashita Year of the Biggest Sales Celebrations, and then to San Francisco for his three-months' leave. Sorry, you'll just have to pine for him; it's your own fault. I warned you not to fall for people like that; they're always on the go, and who knows who they shack up with overseas.'

'You're a bitch, Seini. Anyway, what about Big Ben himself?'

'Haven't you heard? You must be the only one. Well, Big B's in a critical condition at the hospital. He went to the Russian Ambassador's cocktail party the other night, got absolutely drunk, and attacked his own wife. That was a near-fatal mistake; the missis got him on the head with an empty whisky bottle. Serves him right, I say. A lot of other things happened at that cocktail party, you know. The Director of Manpower also got drunk and swore at his Minister who smashed him on the kisser and then got himself kneed in the balls by the Director's wife. Those high-class women are pretty dangerous. And then that old billy goat, Henry Coles, took off with Mrs Cohen to God knows where. Mr Cohen is in Suva conducting a four-week training course. People shouldn't go overseas so often, leaving their wives behind. I don't blame the poor bitches getting it on the sly; they hardly get it straight, poor things. I'd do it myself if I were them.'

'You'll never be one of them,' said Susana, and put down the phone. 'I'm very sorry. There's no one downstairs either. Come back in a month's time.'

Ika went back after a month but couldn't get to see anyone. He returned once more, then gave up trying to see the Appropriate Authorities. And, because of official inaccessibility and his own predilections, Ika fell behind in paying back the loan. He fell so far behind that one day he ceased being frightened, took out his imported dinghy, the Rendo motor, and the six big nets, went two miles out to sea, pulled out an axe and hacked a huge hole in the bottom of the boat. Then he swam slowly ashore, cool and relaxed for the first time in months and months.

He wrote short letters to the Appropriate Authorities and reported regretfully that his boat and equipment were at the bottom of the ocean owing to a most unfortunate accident. Since he had neither money nor anything worth confiscating, and since he could not be held on any legal grounds, no one tried to touch him. His name was simply added to a long, long list of unreliable persons not worth aiding in the future.

Ika couldn't care less, and today you will find him on a certain beach in Tulisi patching up an old dinghy and talking happily with his friends. Not all are so fortunate.

One such less fortunate person was Toa Qase, who was a successful small-time market gardener and banana grower until he switched to big-time chicken farming under the Poultry Development Scheme funded by an agency of the Great International Organisation. Toa abandoned all forms of gardening, obtained a loan, and built a big shed to house six thousand infant chickens flown in from New Zealand.

The chickens grew large and lovely, and Toa's fame spread. Everyone knew he had six thousand chickens and everyone wanted to taste them. A well-bred Tikong gives generously to his relatives and neighbours, especially one with thousands of earthly goods. But under the guidance of a Development Expert, who was Elite and a Wise Man to boot, Toa aimed to become a Modern Businessman, forgetting that in Tiko if you give less you will lose more and if you give nothing you will lose all. And Toa's chickens began to disappear, a dozen on the first night filched by his underpaid chicken-farmhands, two dozen the second night filched by the same underpaid farmhands plus their friends, and so on. Word spread that Toa's chickens were fast disappearing so why not help yourself before they were all gone. Thus everyone who happened to walk by the road at night helped himself to Toa's large and lovely chickens before they were all gone.

As for Toa, he gave up his dream of becoming a wealthy Modern Businessman, bade Godspeed to the Development Expert, and went to his clergyman for consolation and advice. The said Man of God reached for the Good Book, opened at St Matthew and read, 'Lay not up for yourselves treasures upon earth where moth and rust doth corrupt, and where thieves break through and steal.' Yes, Toa remembered, and vowed he would never again be so greedy for earthly goods.

Since then, as Manu tells it, Toa has devoted all his time to developing for himself vast treasures in Heaven where live neither thieves nor experts.

A Pilgrim's Progress

Noeli Ma'a was born in 1941 of sturdy Sabbatarian stock. From the very beginning he was a good lad, the nicest and most obedient in Saisaipē, the village of his proud, productive parents.

Before he knew what was what, Noeli's nanny made him a Lamb in her chapter of the School of Angels, to which belonged all Sabbatarian grandmothers and great-grandmothers in Saisaipē. At the School the ancient and not so ancient women primed themselves for turning into Angels sooner or later when the Lord of Hosts deemed it time to toll their knells and call them Home.

As part of her preparation for the winged, celestial Life Hereafter, Noeli's nanny had to look at and ponder upon visible manifestations of Purity, the most important element in the make-up of an Angel. Teachers of Sunday School say that spotless white lambs are the closest thing on earth to the Soaring Hosts, but there are no lambs in Tiko, which is just as well for sheep here would not keep their whiteness long, on account of too much rain and mud. White lambs abound in Australia, declared the lanky missionary from Sydney, because that country has precious little rain and therefore hardly any mud. White lambs abound in Australia, said Manu, because no sheep of tinted fleece is ever allowed into that spotless land.

That might or might not be, but the truth was that Saisaipē had no lambs, white or tinted, to look at or ponder upon. Pigs and dogs abound by the thousands but, since by nature filthy, they were no good as symbols of Purity. On the other hand little children who knew not what was what, when

27

thoroughly scrubbed, oiled, combed, and dressed, looked cute and could therefore stand for Lambs and Angels.

Thus every second Sunday afternoon Nanny chose her littlest grandchild, Noeli; scrubbed and oiled him from head to toe, plastered his hair, and covered his body with white clothes, white shoes, and a white cap, before herding him to the School's meeting place. There, two dozen Apprentice Angels sat around the walls chanting ancient Psalms and pondering upon their Little Lambs sitting in the middle quietly and contentedly eating lollies. And Noeli was judged by all to be the cutest and the best Little Lamb in the whole of Sai-saipē.

When Noeli entered Primary School and began learning unlamblike things about life on earth and was well on the way to knowing what was what, his grandmother dropped him in favour of his baby brother. She sent Noeli to Sunday School where, as a Hogget, he was told to be good and obedient, and to keep away from Temptation. On the fifth day of Sunday School the following typical exchange took place between the Sunday School teacher and Noeli.

'Noeli,' asked the teacher, 'who was the most obedient child in the Old Testament?'

'Samuel.' Noeli blurted out the correct answer that had literally been slapped into his head over the previous four Sunday School sessions.

'Good boy. And what happened to Samuel?' asked the teacher, raising a cane and swishing the air.

'He was called upon by the Lord one day,' Noeli stuttered in response.

'Very good; you're improving fast. And what was Noeli's, I mean Samuel's, reply to the Lord?' The cane slashed the air three times, expressing the teacher's annoyance more with herself than with anyone else.

'Samuel said, "Speak Lord, for thy servant heareth."'

'Excellent. You must always behave like little Samuel. Who knows but that one day the Lord may actually speak to you. Now, who brings Temptation into the world?'

'Satan,' replied Noeli with mounting confidence.

'And who was the first person in history to be tempted by Satan?'

'Eve, wife of Adam.'

'In what form did Satan appear to Eve?'

'In the form of a snake.'

'Yes, indeed. The snake, children, is an ugly, oily thing. It worms its way into all sorts of things, especially where it shouldn't go. We're lucky there are no snakes in Tiko. We have too many temptations as it is. Now, Noeli, what do you do when Satan comes to you?'

'I fall on my knees and pray to Jesus.'

'Good. And what else do you do to keep Satan at bay?'

'I do exactly as you told me. I sleep with a Bible under my pillow and carry a pocket-sized one wherever I go. This also helps to keep ghosts away.'

'Very good and very obedient of you, Noeli. You keep doing that and you will have no problem getting into Heaven. Now, children, you must always have a Bible wherever you are. And remember that Adam and Eve ate the snake and lost all their clothes because they did not carry their Bibles around with them.'

And so every Sunday afternoon Noeli went to Sunday School where he learnt how to deal with Temptation. He also learnt of the land where lions and lambs play and sleep together, of the good shepherd who became a better king, of the bad king who turned into a leper and lost his throne, and of the holy man who went body and all to Heaven without dying first. There were other tales of good and evil, stories which kept Noeli going happily to Sunday School until he had nearly completed Secondary Schooling, at which stage he had become a Young Ram with growing horns. And then, Bibles under pillows or Bibles in trouser pockets notwithstanding, the horns kept growing.

Up to that stage Noeli had no insoluble problems; all temptations were solved easily and quickly by his Sabbatarian parents and his Sabbatarian Sunday School. Everything went well, smoothly and cleanly, until he developed some ineffably strange inner and outer stirrings which led to his discovery that the Sabbatarian Church, which had provisions for taking care of Little Lambs, Hoggets, and Old Sheep, had nothing for Young Rams and Ewes but Bible Reading, Hymning, and

Praying. Noeli became restless and fidgety, and concluded that the Sabbatarian Church was dull and stodgy and lacking in oomph.

It was then that he began to look this way and that, and lo he saw the Morocs; yes, the Morocs of the Ancient Prophets, with their dance halls and tennis courts, brass bands with pipes and string bands with saxophones.

One day Noeli went to Tulisi to watch the school procession for the Anniversary of Independence. Sabbatarian schools marched behind pious prefects and middle-aged spinsters with tree-trunk legs; other schools did little better or little worse. But the Morocs were a sight; their schools followed Marching Girls in shorts doing unbelievable things with their twirling sticks: throwing them over and around their heads, behind their backs and, best of all, between their legs. And when Noeli saw the Moroc Marching Girls doing things like that his heart went pit-a-pat for a second or two before it jumped and pumped furiously like a runaway oil-rig piston.

But more importantly Noeli's soul danced to the tunes of the Moroc brass and pipes and to the sight of the twirling sticks of the Moroc Marching Girls. His soul never jived to the Sabbatarian brass playing Mr Handel's anthems or the old Tiko tunes. And thus at nineteen, Noeli, whose nanny had long ago joined the Heavenly Band of Angels, decided to follow where his dancing soul led: straight into the warmth and glitter of the Moroc Church of Christ and the Ancient Prophets.

During his first year of conversion Noeli joined the Moroc national brass band, playing a trumpet. He blew that trumpet with all his might, and he huffed and he puffed and he popped his eyes, but he got nowhere close to a Marching Girl, nor even to a twirling stick. He tried harder the second year, but the Marching Girls pranced ahead twirling their sticks, giving him not a wink of recognition.

Noeli's soul became restless again. It still danced to the tunes of the Moroc brass and pipes, but it did it solo which was no damn good. His soul must have a dancing partner or it would wither and die. But the trouble was that the face on the body that housed Noeli's soul was splattered with pimples, which meant the Moroc Marching Girls didn't look at him.

One day, while window-shopping in Tulisi, Noeli happened upon a group of teenagers singing and preaching at a street corner. Eight lovely lasses and six handsome lads there were in that little band of Apostolics. As they stood singing and swaying their youthful bodies in harmony with each other and with the Lord, Noeli's soul leapt and swung in mid-air, feeling sensations it had never before experienced. Oh, the joy! The Gates of Heaven had suddenly and briefly opened, allowing Noeli a peep into Eternal Ecstasy. And when the leading lass stepped forward calling for Conversion and Acceptance of the Saviour, Noeli let his leaping soul march him out of the Moroc fold into the arms of the Apostolic Church, and hopefully into those of its pretty preachers.

Noeli found the new faith very much to his liking. With the Morocs, the brass band was always twenty yards from the rear ends of the Marching Girls, which was too far for anything nice to happen. With the Apostolics, on the other hand, everyone stood tightly packed on the street corner, arms, hips, and legs rubbing in closed-eyed, swaying harmony to the tunes and the rhythms of hymns from the sweet Bible Belt of the USA.

Twice a week Noeli stood on Tulisi street corners with the little band of Apostolic witnesses, placing himself between two girls, Lisi and Mina, and very pretty and clean Young Ewes they were. Noeli's left arm, hip, and leg swayed and rubbed against those of Lisi, while his right limbs moved with those of Mina. He became fervent, and he sang and cried and shouted and preached the Gospel. Heavens above, he thought, this is Eternal Ecstasy! And every so often the spirit of love and joy would possess him, and his knees would buckle and he would fall and for a split second his eyes would scan the swaying thighs of Lisi and Mina and he would shake deliciously before passing out. That happened twice a week and Noeli loved every moment of it.

One afternoon he swooned and fell face up, eyes agog and

head resting on the pavement and incidentally between Lisi's lovely legs. He screamed with joy and glee and made to rise. Lisi screeched and put a foot none too gently on Noeli's pimply face. Nothing seemed amiss but at the following session Noeli found himself firmly planted between two burly Apostolic boys. And every session thereafter Noeli tried to get in between Lisi and Mina but somehow always found himself flanked by the two biggest boys in the group.

This is no damn good, thought Noeli sadly. And once again he became restless and fidgety, for he detested swaying with the boys; Lord be his witness, his soul was straight and anyone with half an eye could see that; clear as a sunny day. But clouds of gloom hung over Noeli's days and his Apostolic fervour began to wane and wither and he eventually dropped out altogether. But he was still a strong believer, pining for a more accommodating faith, and for a dancing partner for his lonely soul.

One fine morning as he was about to give up all hope of attaining Eternal Ecstasy he stumbled upon a group of street-corner preachers representing the Gatherings for God, a more progressive set of evangelists than you would find elsewhere in Tiko. The group had a string band complete with guitars, a tambourine, and booming loudspeakers, and played hymns sung to Country & Western tunes. To appeal more to the souls of worldly-wise Tulisians, the Gatherings recruited their workers from the ranks of senior students from Tiko High School and sang all their songs in English.

One such evangelist was Kali Momona, a beautiful ex-Sabbatarian lass of twenty who had sat three times for her University Entrance Examination without success on account of her spending too much time witnessing on the street corners of Tulisi. Heavenly Wisdom, said Kali, was more precious than all the earthly knowledge one could gather. And Heaven bestowed upon Kali the skill of playing the group's tambourine as that instrument had never been played before. Instead of shaking it in any old way, Kali appeared to caress it, while in truth she applied the method of Dynamic Tension, producing a haunting, ethereal strain that sounded like the whine of a sick Angel.

People flocked to hear the weird sound of Kali's tambourine, but Noeli was more concerned with the music in Kali's soul. As he looked through her into the beauty of her loveliness, and as he contemplated her other potentials, Noeli's soul quivered and flipped, to say the least. And hardly had the music ended than Noeli had accepted the call for Conversion for the third time in his young life, pledging himself to be a faithful follower and witness of the Gatherings for God. He bought a guitar and joined the band of street-corner student-evangelists, playing next to Kali. This time around Noeli's prayers were answered, for his pimples were disappearing and his own beauty, so long submerged, was beginning to surface and shine.

One day, in the heat of spiritual enchantment, Kali cried out, 'I love you, Lord Jesus!'

'Hallelujah; and I love you too, my darling.'

Kali turned to face the Lord, only to confront Noeli's hopeful grin. 'Stop that nonsense at once, you silly idiot. I'm grabbed by the spirit.'

'And so am I. But I'm also grabbed by you, my beloved.'

'Grab yourself. I love only Jesus.'

'I do too, yes I do. But I also think of you all the time.'

'Look here,' Kali hissed, 'this is a religious event, and you're being sacrilegious. My love's all spiritual, anyway.'

'Mine too, so help me Lord. It's all so spiritual. My soul's in love with yours. Will you marry me ?'

'Shut up, fart face. And stop rubbing your leg on mine. Come into my heart, Lord Jesus! Take me to your bosom! Hallelujah, I love the Lord!' Kali declared to the universe.

But more than the Lord did Kali end up loving. Although she had been approached many times by many men of many shapes she had never been wooed in the middle of a religious celebration. Noeli's unorthodox approach astounded her; but then, she said to herself, what's more fitting for a fervent Christian than to be courted in a prayerful setting? Perhaps the Almighty had sent him to her. She began to look seriously at Noeli, and discovered him increasingly attractive. And pretty soon she found herself playing her tambourine in time to his guitar.

As weeks of witnessing went by, the sounds of the guitar and the tambourine merged and parted in unison and harmony while the souls of their players danced in silent ecstasy. And before very long, Noeli and Kali, who also did things not altogether spiritual, sealed their all in Holy Matrimony.

They continued working for the Gatherings, witnessing in Tulisi and elsewhere, but the time came when they arrived at the Old Sheep stage that required a quieter, more reflective life than they had led. The Gatherings, they felt, had too much energy and too many restless Rams with growing horns and itchy Ewes with thickening wool. And standing for long periods on street corners, however worthy the cause, put too much strain on weakening legs and flagging strength.

Noeli and Kali therefore began looking for a faith that had as little life as possible, settling on the old Sabbatarian Church which, they joyfully decided, was as ever dull and stodgy and lacking in oomph. But, as Manu pointed out, the Sabbatarian Church offered a refuge for Ageing Rams and Ewes, and a golden gateway to Life Hereafter through its fantastic and unique institution, the Holy School of Angels.

The Wages of Sin

Ti Pilo Siminī is a weedy little man who smokes continuously except when asleep. He smokes so much he often forgets that he already has a cigarette in his mouth and proceeds to light another one, the result being that he is the only person anywhere who may be seen with two or even three cigarettes stuck between his lips. Doctors at the National Hospital say that he should have died from lung cancer long before he turned thirty, but Ti is sixty-seven and has never had so much as a cough in his life.

When Ti runs out of tobacco he begs some from the first person he sees, and will even ask for the cigarette he is smoking. Every smoker in Tulisi ducks at the sight of him; no one wants to meet or even see him. But, like a Tikong ghost, Ti cannot be avoided; people stumble upon him when and where they least expect to do so, each departing at least one cigarette poorer.

And when Ti walks the untidy streets of Tulisi he not only sees everyone who looks, acts, and smells like a smoker, his eyes also scan every inch of the ground for cigarette butts, which he picks up and drops into a dirty little bag he carries everywhere he goes. Every morning at the dawn of pigs he prowls around people's homes in search of cigarette butts. Every day at lunch-time he haunts the grounds of junior secondary schools, confiscating cigarettes from little boys smoking their heads off in hiding places he knows so well, though teachers of junior secondary schools do not.

Every night Ti wakes at regular intervals to have a smoke before resuming his sleep. One night he stirred at two o'clock. The house was pitch dark but Ti was too lazy to rise and light the lamp. He groped in the dark for his tobacco bag, found it, but after investigation discovered that there were no cigarette papers. Again he groped in the dark, fumbled here and there before he found a book, opened it, ripped out a page with which he rolled a cigarette, smoked happily, then drifted off to sleep.

And he dreamed a dreadful dream. Moses, the lawgiver of Israel, appeared with his trusted lieutenant Joshua at his side. Looking very angry, Moses pointed a finger at Ti saying, 'Ti Pilo Siminī, you have committed an act of sacrilege for which you will be punished severely. Joshua! Attend to the offender!'

'Aye, aye, sir!' replied Joshua, advancing upon the trembling Ti and pulling out a stick of dynamite from his armpit. He forced one end of the explosive into Ti's mouth, lit the fuse, and quickly disappeared with Moses into thin air. The dynamite exploded and Ti woke up screaming at the top of his voice. He could not resume his sleep and spent the rest of the night figuring out what act of sacrilege he had committed.

It was not until the break of dawn, when he reached for his Bible to read a passage before saying his morning prayer, that he discovered the terrible thing he had done. The Holy Book lay open on the floor with a page ripped out. The missing leaf was that which contained the Ten Commandments. In Tiko, damaging the Holy Book is an act of sacrilege, but burning it had never been heard of. A Tikong will commit with impunity any number of sins, but he will never deface the Good Book, let alone send it up in smoke.

With the full realisation of the enormity of his sin, Ti knelt on the floor and prayed for two hours, asking God's forgiveness and promising to replace the missing leaf by the following morning. He spent the rest of the day inside his house, speaking to no one and drawing not a single puff, so great was his fear. As word spread that Ti had for once confined himself to his house, happy smokers filled the streets of Tulisi and, in hiding places on the grounds of junior secondary schools, little boys puffed away, stunting their growth and damaging their tiny brains with joyful abandon.

Darkness fell but Ti did not stir. At midnight, however,

when even dogs were fast asleep, Ti emerged from his house, crept to that of his neighbour, entered it, searched around carefully, found his neighbour's Holy Book, removed the leaf containing the Ten Commandments, hurried home, pasted the stolen item into his own Bible, smiled happily, and went straight to bed.

And he dreamed a terrible dream. Moses, the great lawgiver, reappeared with the faithful Joshua at his side. If Moses had been very angry the previous evening, this time around he was furious. 'Ti Pilo Siminī!' he roared, 'you have committed two acts of sacrilege and one act of theft. Damn you! Joshua! Attend to the offender!'

'Aye, aye, sir!' responded Joshua, advancing upon the trembling Ti and pulling out two sticks of dynamite from his armpit. He forced them into Ti's mouth, lit the fuse, and took two steps back to where Moses was standing. The lawgiver and his faithful lieutenant were so furious that they forgot to disappear into thin air. As the dynamite exploded upon all three of them, Ti woke up screaming twice as loudly as he had the previous night, and stayed awake through to sunrise, shaking from head to toe.

On the following morning he prayed for three hours, begging the Lord for forgiveness and promising to restore the stolen Holy Leaf to its rightful owner. Once again Ti spent the day inside his house speaking to no one and puffing not a single puff. Once again unaccosted smokers filled the streets of Tulisi and in hiding places on the grounds of junior secondary schools little boys inflicted more damage upon their tiny brains with blissful unconcern.

At midnight, when even mosquitoes had ceased humming, Ti emerged from his house and crept to that of his neighbour, clutching the pilfered Holy Leaf. He entered, groping his way across the room, and by chance landing his hands on something soft, warm, and moving. He examined it thoroughly and discovered the object of his fingerwork to be the reclining, responding figure of his neighbour's spouse, who was totally unclad. And, as any healthy male Tikong would have done under similar circumstances, Ti forgot his penitent mission and proceeded at once to deal with the matter at hand,

and botched the job. Upon which occasion the hitherto yield-
ing spouse, a lady of vast dimensions, rose to her feet, lifted
Ti by the scruff of his neck, screamed rape, and deposited a
mighty fist with such force upon his jaw that he flew across
the room, crashed through the thin coconut-leaf wall, landed
heavily outside, managed somehow to pull himself together,
and staggered home still clutching the stolen Holy Leaf.

On entering his house Ti passed out and dreamed the worst
dream yet. Moses and his dutiful Joshua appeared. If the great
jurist had been furious the previous night, he was now livid,
and his whole body shook with barely-controlled rage, which
was not surprising, for as a result of the dynamite explosion
most of his body was wrapped in bandages, Band-Aids, and
slings. Being a much younger man and a ferocious warrior,
Joshua was better off than his mentor; the worst he had got
was a smashed eye and a lost tooth—which dampened his
fury none. 'An eye for an eye and a tooth for a tooth,' he
mumbled under his breath, glowering at Ti.

On seeing the two dreadful apparitions Ti shook as he had
never shaken before. He was so seized with fright that he lost
control of his bodily functions and presently felt some warm
fluid coursing down his thighs. He grabbed for the offend-
ing region, succeeding only in getting his hands wet.

'Ti Pilo Siminī!' Moses thundered, 'you have committed
three acts of sacrilege, one act of theft, one act of prevarication, one act of unlawful fornication, and one act of botchery.
God damn you! Joshua! Attend to the offender!'

'Aye, aye, sir!' Joshua bellowed back; then advanced upon
the trembling, wetting Ti, extracted three sticks of dynamite
from his armpit, forced them into Ti's mouth, lit the fuse,
and was about to inflict something horrible upon Ti's decrepit
person when Moses grabbed his arm and they made to vanish
into the thin air. And when all but their legs had disappeared,
the dynamite exploded. Ti woke up screaming at the top of
his voice and would not return to sleep lest he dreamed again.

In the morning Ti prayed for four hours, begging the Lord
for forgiveness and promising to redeem himself by the following sunrise. He remained in his house, speaking to no one
and lighting not a single cigarette. But out on the dusty streets

of Tulisi drunken smokers pranced and puffed, and in hiding places on the grounds of junior secondary schools little boys smoked away their chances of ever again passing an examination.

At midnight, when even the stars had ceased blinking, Ti took the stolen Holy Leaf, went out of his house, and crept to that of his neighbour. A few yards from his destination he stopped dead, for his neighbour's front door crashed open and out staggered his neighbour's son. Ti gathered his wits in time and dived into a hole dug by his neighbour's pigs. Sonny staggered to the edge of the hole, unzipped his trousers, and embarked upon creating a duck-pond with the three cartons of beer he had been drinking all day and half the night. Caught in the torrential downpour, Ti moved his hands to shield his face and in doing so dropped the pilfered Holy Leaf, which promptly dissolved in the deluge. And when he realised what had happened to the object of his mission Ti cried 'Piss off!', rose, and ran like hell.

His neighbour's son was so astounded by what had transpired under his very nozzle that in a flash he pulled up his zipper, catching his tenderness in the process, howled with searing pain, stumbled, and fell into the pool Ti had just vacated. Unleashing a string of evil words, Sonny rose, disentangled and recircumcised himself in the process, howled again, and sped after Ti, searing the night with filthy language. To cut a long story short, suffice it to say that after a roundabout chase of half an hour Ti weaved his way home, where he collapsed into insensibility.

And he dreamed a dream such as he would never have imagined. Moses and his trusted Joshua appeared, both in wheelchairs on account of the dynamite exploding under their legs the night before, and stopped two hundred yards from Ti. Behind them ranged the entire Israeli Armed Forces, all set to administer the dreaded Begin Blitz upon Ti should Moses again be harmed, however slightly. And when he saw the mightiest fighting forces of the Middle East ranged against his lonely Tikong self, Ti shook, screamed, and squeezed his thighs to no good purpose before he fell and fainted.

Upon regaining consciousness he heard a hundred trumpets flourish and a hundred drums of war roll, after which the voice of Moses came booming through an amplifier: 'Ti Pilo Siminī! You have committed five acts of sacrilege, one act of theft, one act of prevarication, one act of unlawful fornication, one act of botchery, three acts of grievous bodily harm, one act of using filthy language, and two acts of polluting the national park. To hell with you! Samson! Attend to the offender!'

'Aye, aye, sir!' boomed Samson, who had replaced the disabled Joshua. He advanced toward Ti, nailed him to a cross, extracted four sticks of dynamite from his armpit, forced them into Ti's mouth, let out a long string as he backed to where Moses and the Israeli Forces were stationed, lit the fuse, and vanished into thin air along with everyone but Ti. Two minutes later when the dynamite exploded upon his crucified self, Ti woke up screaming as he had the previous evening, only more so. He stayed up to sunrise, vowing never ever again to close his eyes.

Next morning he prayed for five hours, begging forgiveness, pledging nothing in advance, on account of what had happened to his other promises. And although he desperately needed advice on how to handle himself the coming evening he could not go to his clergyman, who would most certainly excommunicate him on the spot; nor could he go to any of his relatives, for they were, without exception, unrepentant sinners and out of divine favour. It was then that he remembered his only true friend, Manu. Of course, he said to himself, why did he not think of Manu days ago?

Ti however remained in his house, communicating with no one, not even with a cigarette. At midnight, when nice ladies had done their last leak for the evening, he emerged from his house, stole to a certain beach and woke Manu, who was sleeping on the sand. When Ti finished telling him everything about his tribulations Manu considered him silently for a while before laying a comforting hand on his shoulder, saying soothingly, 'Ti, you have really done some stupid things and have deserved your punishment. But don't worry, my friend. The solution to your problem is simple. Go home and smoke a cigarette rolled in another Holy Leaf.'

'But that's how the trouble started in the first place!' Ti protested. 'I won't do it! I don't want five sticks of dynamite exploding in my mouth! Keep your advice to yourself, thank you.'

'No thank you. Listen to me,' Manu insisted. 'You see, a negative and a negative make a positive. Likewise, a sin can only be cancelled by an equal and opposite sin.'

'But I have committed many without them cancelling each other; and look at what has happened! Dear God.'

'Yes, He is,' Manu responded calmly. 'But your sins couldn't cancel each other because they weren't equal and opposite.'

'What are you talking about?' asked Ti, who had never heard anything so mysterious. Manu declined to respond, for the question raised tricky theological issues and Ti had had no training at the Tiko Bible College.

'Ti?' Manu broke the ensuing silence. 'Have I ever, ever failed you?'

'No, not until just now,' Ti replied,

'That's arguable. But, let's not dwell on it. If I suggest the only possible solution to your problem, will you do it?'

Ti didn't want to do it but, seeing that it was long past midnight, with no alternative advice forthcoming from any other quarter, replied, 'Yes, I will. And it had better be the right solution or you will lose a dear friend.'

'O.K. Now listen carefully. Go home, rip out the Holy Leaf containing St Luke Chapter Twenty-Three, Verse Thirty-Four. Roll a cigarette in it and have a smoke before you go to bed. Do it with the right leaf or you will have five sticks of dynamite up your Netherlands. O Lord. It could only happen to you. Go now. And good luck.'

Ti rose heavily, returned to his house and, although near panic, tore the prescribed Holy Leaf from the Good Book. He perused the relevant verse, rolled a cigarette, smoked, at first hesitantly then ravenously, drifted off to sleep, and dreamed.

Moses appeared with Joshua at his side, stopping two hundred yards away and sitting on wheelchairs held by Samson and Goliath. Behind them ranged the combined Zionist-Palestinian Peace-Keeping Forces which, on a signal from

Samson, flourished a hundred trumpets and rolled a hundred drums of war. Then the voice of Moses came booming through the loudspeaker: 'Ti Pilo Siminī! You have committed six acts of sacrilege, one act of theft, one act of unlawful fornication, one act. . . .' But Moses paused as someone materialised at his side. He was beautiful, sweet, and divine.

'Moses, Moses,' said the newcomer, 'put that microphone away will you?'

Moses promptly complied, saying, 'At once, sir.'

'Thank you,' responded the newcomer, advancing upon the trembling offender. 'Ti Pilo Siminī, you have done many awful things and have deserved all your punishment. But you have also committed an act of equal and opposite sin which has cancelled all your other transgressions. Go home and sin no more.'

'Yes, sir; thank you, thank you,' Ti responded gratefully, falling on his knees.

'Sir?' he ventured shortly, 'what is an equal and opposite sin?'

The newcomer looked at Ti, pointed a forgiving finger upward, and replied, 'I will explain it to you, my son, if you care to come to my abode. For a cup of tea, perhaps? And something to smoke, maybe?'

Ti rose, vanished with the newcomer into thin air, and materialised at a celestial mansion where he drank a delicious cup of tea and smoked a heavenly cigar. And the newcomer revealed to him the secrets of life and death and wisdom.

From that night on Ti has never sinned a single sin. Instead he always commits two simultaneously, one the equal and opposite of the other.

Paths to Glory

My son, said Tevita Poto's uncle, scrutinising with right-eous distaste his nephew's unkempt appearance, listen to me. You've returned from the lands of learning and wealth. You've brought home great wisdom, to the joy of the whole of Tiko and the pride of our Family. And you've been here for five years, have you not? Yet it is apparent to me and to all that in those years you have not done any great deed, you have not served His Excellency's Government, the Church of God on Earth, or even our humble Family.

What has happened to your learning? What has happened to the many degrees you brought home to Tiko? You're so clever and so full of knowledge. But what is the matter with you? Have our prayers gone unheard? Has the labour of your father and grandfathers been to no avail?

Look at you. Is that the appearance of a Man of Many Degrees? Is that how Wise Men should look? Your hair is long and uncombed; your beard is bushy and scruffy; your clothes, your clothes are those of foolish folk. You should show respect for your great learning; you should wear clean and spotless clothes; and you should look respectable as should a Man of Many Degrees.

You walk around like a fool; you walk around like Manu. That's humility taken too far and no one respects you for it. Lower yourself by all means; be meek and be gentle, but at appropriate times. It's a matter of timing, my son. You're not an ordinary man; you're Elite and you should walk like one and act like one. As of now your appearance shames the Family.

What's more, my son, why do you criticise the Government so much? Why do you criticise the Church so much? You say you want to speak the truth. What's the use of truth in Tiko? Will truth change anything? Will truth make you tall? Will it make anyone rich? Will truth be believed in Tiko?

If you stand with the truth, opposed by His Excellency and the Great Chiefs, Tiko will grind you small. That's the truth about our land, my son. Forget the Law and forget the Constitution. It's the will of His Excellency and the Great Chiefs that makes things move in Tiko; it's the will of His Excellency and the Great Chiefs that makes things not move in Tiko. Never forget that.

Go forth then and work for the Government, serve God, and forget about truth. Truth is foreign thinking, and this is Tiko. Truth and Tiko don't relate, and you of all people should know that.

Another thing, my son. Go to Church every Sunday; go to Church. For many generations our Family has worked for the Church, has suffered for the Church, has died for the Church. You got your education and your degrees through the power of generations of service and prayer to Jehovah. Don't ever think that you got them by your own efforts alone. Never, never, my son. Your great learning is the reward for the good work of the whole Family since True Religion arrived in Tiko. God rewards those who believe in Him, who serve Him well and faithfully.

You say the Church is not Christian and you say the Church is useless. How can that be so? How can a Christian Church be not Christian? What manner of thinking is that? What kind of foreigners taught you woolly thoughts? And how can the Church be useless? The Church is God's creation and God's creations are never useless!

Believe in God, my son; go to Church and obey His Chairman. God selected His Chairman, and the Chairman is a good man, the Chairman is a great man and the Chairman is a prophet. God never chooses buffoons and hypocrites to be Chairmen of His Churches! No, no, never! God bless His Chairmen everywhere! And God bless His Churches everywhere!

Dear, oh dear, you make me so cross. One last thing. Take my word, son. You have been away from Tiko for far too long. Yes, you have been away far too long for your own good, for the good of Tiko, the Church, and the Family. You think like a foreigner, you talk like a foreigner, and you act like a foreigner.

For instance, you're not just you, as you've said so often; that's foreign thinking. You're of the Family, and the Family is of you. If you walk well the Family is proud; if you stumble the Family is ashamed. If you prosper the Family rises, but if you squander your talents the Family will remain poor. The Family looks to you because you're the pinnacle of its achievement.

You must therefore shed your foreign thinking. You must shed your foreign ways in order to lead the proper life here, in order to be of service to God, to His Excellency, and to the Family. Remember that this is Tiko, and you must re-learn the ways of Tiko. That is all for now, my son. Good-bye, God bless you. And don't forget to cut your hair.

My son, said Tevita Poto's father, an active evangelist of forty years standing, look here and answer my questions. What was the topic of the sermon last Sunday? You don't know? Didn't you go to Church last Sunday? What about the Sunday before? And the one before that? Have you not been to Church since your return? A few times only? Why? Say it again? But you have to go to Church whether you feel like it or not! What do you think Sundays are for?

Now answer the next questions straight and truthfully. I know you have answered my questions truthfully! How could anyone say what you've just said and be lying at the same time?

Do you still read the Bible? Only for historical reference? But that's sacrilege! Don't you know the Bible is not a history book? The Bible is the Word of God! What kind of foreigners led you astray, you stupid shit-eater! Look at what you've done to me.

Do you pray every morning and night? Don't you pray at all? But why? Why you of all people? Have I not raised you in the shadow of Jesus? Have I not prayed for you twice daily since you were born?

Do you believe in God? No, no, don't answer that ques-

45

tion; it might make me swear again. Now listen carefully, my son. It matters not a farthing how much learning you have had; it matters not a cent how many degrees you have acquired; if you don't accept Christ as your Saviour you will not amount to anything.

Look at you. You don't look like a Man of Many Degrees. You look like Manu, and you act like Manu. You're scruffy! You're ridiculous! And your pipe smells like rotten fish! People laugh at you and you don't care because you're so selfish. You never think of our Family. But the Family is ashamed and so am I. You've done nothing in the five years you've been here. You will never do anything worthwhile unless you open your heart to Jesus Christ.

And one last thing. How long have you been married? Twenty years? Well. And how many children have you got? That's your just desert! You see, children are God's reward to those who believe in Him. He will never entrust His little ones to unbelievers. Pray to Him, beg His forgiveness and mercy, and surrender, surrender completely to Him. It's your last chance. Mark my words!

I beg your pardon, doctor, said the tipsy taxi driver standing beside Tevita Poto at the bar of the Tiko Club. You're a Wise Man and a Scholar, and I'm uneducated and ignorant. But, begging your pardon, why do you Wise Men always sit up there looking down on us? Why don't you ever come down to our level?

Well it makes no difference that you're always here drinking beer with us. And I don't believe you saying that you don't belong up there, that you belong nowhere, and that you are just you. You belong up there with the rest of those educated bastards. You deny it because you're trying to be humble. Shit! You earn more money than most Tikongs. You work for foreigners. Aha! So you work for the Pacific Region. Not with those crazy guys hawking the Pacific Way? Is that so? Good Lord, forget it! This is Tiko! It's not the bloody Pacific Region! The Pacific Way belongs to regional Elites, Experts, Wheeler-dealers, and Crooks! And Tiko is in Tiko! So what if Tiko is in the Pacific? Don't change the subject!

You say, doctor, that all men are equal. How can you say that when you're so rich and I'm so poor? I beg your pardon, please, I'm uneducated and ignorant.

Hey, barman, give the professor another bottle; and the same for me. Write it down barman, write it down—I'll pay you tomorrow. Shut up! I'm talking to a Wise Man.

Where were we? Yes; and another thing. Why did you say that mutton flap is dangerous rubbish and Tiko is the garbage dump of New Zealand? You're a Wise Man and a Rich Man. Ignorant Men are poor. You eat eggs and bacon for breakfast and fillet steak for dinner. We can only afford mutton flap. So what if you don't eat eggs and bacon for breakfast and fillet steak for dinner? That's beside the point. The truth is that you, doctor, can afford to buy those things any time; and you can afford to go around saying nasty things about mutton flap. You can buy the world, but we can only take the flap. We eat and love it. It's a matter of getting used to what you can buy.

And one more thing. You are so fond of talking about democracy. Democracy is a foreign idea. You Wise Men are for ever bringing in foreign things. This is Tiko, doctor. Democracy and Tiko don't dance, and you're a rich man trying to look poor. You're a hypocrite, if you'll pardon me. Let me tell you this. Democracy in Tiko is most difficult to get. You will have to earn it the hard way, and you will get it not in this life; not here anyway. Pray to God and you will have your democracy in Heaven. Goodbye, professor, I'm off to New Zealand tomorrow. Yes, for good.

And take this loving advice, intoned the Family spokesman at the feast five years ago celebrating Tevita Poto's triumphant return. Go forth and serve the Government and the Church with all your strength, with all your heart, and with all your mind. The Almighty and His Excellency will shortly make you the Minister of Money, and we, your humble Family, will become rich!

The Second Coming

On the day Tiko gained her independence from the shackles of colonialism His Excellency the Paramount Chief proclaimed in no uncertain terms the immediate cessation of all undue exploitation of the citizens and resources of the balmy isles by the running dogs of Imperialism and Capitalism. In the Historical Proclamation, which has since been immortalised in five fine songs composed by Tiko's most eminent wordsmiths, His Excellency also laid down many other wise edicts, but the one which held Sailosi Atiu's attention, raised his hopes, and has since guided his destiny, as well as that of his beloved country, was the statement that henceforth the direction of National Development towards Tiko taking its rightful place among the nations of the Free World would rest in indigenous hands and no others.

Immediately following the Historical Proclamation came the localisation of every post and position that could conceivably be localised, including all the major offices of the realm, except those of the Ministries of Justice and Finance, since it was well nigh impossible to locate suitable candidates of just and honest disposition. The stage was thus set for Tiko to skin her own pigs and so control her Manifest Destiny.

At that time Sailosi Atiu had been working as the chief assistant to the imperial running dog Mr Eric Hobsworth-Smith, Director of the Bureau for the Preservation of Traditional Culture and Essential Indigenous Personality. Mr Hobsworth-Smith was a graduate in anthropology and prehistoric archaeology from the University of London, where he had read all there was to be read on the habits and peculiarities of native peoples in Africa, Asia, the Americas, and Oceania. Following his graduation he entered the Colonial Service and worked for many years as Museum Director, Government Anthropologist, and Special Adviser on Native Affairs in a dozen far-flung countries of the Great British Empire. Nine years before Tiko's independence Mr Hobsworth-Smith arrived to establish and direct the Bureau for the Preservation of Traditional Culture and Essential Indigenous Personality or, more precisely, what remained of these after the running dogs had done their bit for more than a century.

Having not been educated abroad, Sailosi Atiu had no diploma or university degree, but at the time of Mr Hobsworth-Smith's arrival he had gained the kind of experience few men in Tiko could match: he had worked in every government department and agency in the course of twenty years, accumulating valuable intimate knowledge of the inner workings of the colonial administration and of the major and minor indiscretions of every highly placed civil servant. More importantly Sailosi had the right consanguineal connections through his late mother to Tiko's ancient aristocracy. His suitability for the post of Deputy Director of the Bureau was recognised publicly when Their Excellencies the Imperial Governor and the Paramount Chief jointly selected him for the office with minimum fuss: all opposition to his appointment was squashed in the usual manner.

Although Sailosi considered Mr Hobsworth-Smith an unredeemable running dog, he now confesses that he had learned much, nay, too much from him. Through the nine years of subordinate association, Sailosi had so emulated his style of work, dress, speech, and deportment that his friends took to addressing him by the Englishman's name. Most of his peers had received their education in America, Australia, and New Zealand and had adopted the habits and peculiarities of those countries and, seeing the ways in which they conducted and comported themselves, Sailosi was glad that he looked and sounded like a true Briton. Indeed he carried himself so much like Mr Hobsworth-Smith that the Imperial Governor often took him for a cultured English gentleman of impeccable lineage, or so the Governor would exclaim in a tone that was only just perceptibly questioning. Sailosi was never quite certain of the Governor's compliments, although he swallowed them easily enough, especially when they were accompanied by gallons of the good Governor's booze at His Excellency's frequently held cocktail parties, to which Sailosi was regularly invited.

Soon after the great Historical Proclamation, Mr Hobsworth-Smith received his marching orders and Sailosi his inevitable elevation to the exalted post of Director of the Bureau. And, as was then fashionable in the heat of immediate post-independence nationalistic fervour, Sailosi moved quickly to purge himself of all pernicious imperial influences and embarked upon the restoration and preservation of his essential indigenous personality. He dropped his posh accent and spoke English only when necessary and with the distinctive Tikong lilt. He stopped spicing his vernacular conversations with fancy English words and discarded his safari shirt, shorts, and long socks in favour of the national attire, varied with Tiki Togs, Afro-shirts, and other Third World clothes. Finally, with much wrenching of the heart, he abandoned his New Zealand paramour and picked a local lady of wandering inclinations to be his secret friend for life.

But he kept the concrete house, the Kelvinator refrigerator, and the Holden station wagon he had inherited from his predecessor, maintained his membership of the expatriate-dominated Tiko Club and his subscriptions to *Playboy* and *Time* magazines, paid regular visits to the International Nightlight Hotel to dine on grilled steaks and imported potato washed down with French wines, and sent his sons to the special school for the children of the elite and his only daughter to an upper-class convent in Perth. And, since he wore his conscience lightly and avoided thinking of contradictions, he saw no irony whatever in the inconsistency in his life-style. Like his close friends Hiti George VI and Sione Falesi, Sailosi was blessed with freedom from the kind of neurosis which arises from over-sensitivity to contradiction, doubt, or guilt.

Having partly cleansed himself of foreign influences and half-restored his essential indigenous personality, Sailosi set about doing the same to his staff and countrymen. He walked into his office building one morning and stopped at the typist's desk. 'Amelia,' he said sternly, 'go to the back at once and wipe off that silly lipstick. I don't want to see you or anyone else in this bureau wearing lipstick. It's a foul foreign custom. While you're at it, get rid of the French perfume too; it smells froggy. Use the great Tikong all-purpose coconut oil. And is that a smear of talcum powder on your cheeks? Wipe that off too; and don't use it again, it won't turn your skin white.

'Aisea. Yes, you. Did I just hear you say something in English? Don't you ever again use the words "bloody" or "shit" within my hearing. If you have to swear, do it in Tikong; we have hundreds of filthy words you can choose from.

'And you, Kolo. Go shave off that stupid moustache. You look like a foreign sex maniac.

'Now listen, all of you. Every morning I shall tell you what things we must banish from our lives; and I shall do this until I'm satisfied that we have cleansed ourselves of the imperialist taint and have re-established our true Tikong selves. Get back to your work.'

Sailosi's first deputy director was a young university graduate whom he considered over-talented and miseducated. The deputy was so keen on reforming everything at once that when he found himself repeatedly blocked, mostly by Sailosi, he turned bitter and set out to undermine his superior using innuendo and ridicule as his weapons. One day Sailosi overheard him saying, 'That old fossil's a reactionary, half-educated nitwit.' Sailosi never forgave him for that.

'I don't mind one bit his calling me a reactionary,' he confided to his wife in bed that evening. 'It's in the nature of my job to be reactionary. How else can we preserve our culture?'

'Quite so,' responded his wife, 'I agree with you two hundred per cent. But I wish you'd react towards me sometimes. You hardly ever do nowadays.'

'We're too old for that sort of nonsense. I don't mind him calling me half-educated either. That pleases me, in fact. You don't need fancy certificates to sit on top chairs. All these youngsters coming out of the universities are a pathetic lot;

they're so transparent. I rather enjoy lording it over them.'

'Quite so, I agree with you two hundred per cent. But I wish you were lording it over me too; you know, like you used to.'

'Do you have to be so silly? But what I can't stomach is his calling me a nitwit. That's disrespectful, to put it mildly. And it's slur on our family connections. I shall teach him a lesson he will never forget.'

'Quite so, I agree with you two hundred per cent. How about giving me one I will never forget? Agh, not like that, you half-educated nitwit!'

For the following twelve months Sailosi set out purposefully to put his deputy firmly in place. He overlooked recommending his salary rise, dealt with his requests only when too late, said yes to him when he meant no and, most of the time, ignored his presence in the office. And when the deputy resigned and emigrated to Honolulu, Sailosi snorted that he had abandoned his country for personal enrichment.

The second deputy director, another young university graduate, fared no better under Sailosi. And after only six months on the job he went to Auckland to attend a seminar and forgot to return. He even forgot to send in his resignation.

As a result Sailosi studiously avoided having any over-talented, miseducated Tikong on his staff. And as he was a member of the most important committees in the realm, including the loving Public Service Board, he succeeded in converting his powerful friends to the wisdom of looking out for and re-educating the wrongly schooled fellow-indigenes in their ranks. But instead of receiving the directives of their elders with open arms, the skilled and the talented fled the country. 'So what?' exploded the unrepentant Sailosi. 'What's the use of having our own professionals and technicians if all they're interested in is more pay, changing our sacred traditions, and destroying our essential indigenous personality? Let them go. If they think the country will fall without them, they're wrong. We don't need them!'

Events soon vindicated Sailosi's uncompromising stand. At about that time the former imperial countries, having lost the world, developed pangs of conscience for their past over-enjoyment of native peoples everywhere. They also felt so depressed when natives took to dancing lascivious twists to the sound and the rhythms of the balalaika that they started sending underpaid volunteers on bicycles and overpaid experts and emissaries in limousines to the former colonies to right the wrongs and to recapture their fickle affections. And the Great International Organisation, established to provide first-class employment for the excess, over-educated elites of destitute lands, also developed a sense of guilt and assigned its employees for short periods to the capitals and five-star hotels of the Third World instead of confining them to the sterilised, air-conditioned comfort of New York, Paris, and Geneva.

Thus the vacancies created by the flight of over-skilled Tikongs were filled with alacrity by alien experts, technical advisers, volunteers, and Third World elite employees of the Great International Organisation. Grabbed by the spirit of the times, the sin-sick, senile Sabbatarian Church, which had been acting in the merry fashion of dirty old men, also set about exiling its dissident pastors and teachers, replacing them with holy tools from abroad. There was no dearth of expatriates ready to descend on the realm to delocalise and deindigenise it. Foreigners came ever so cheap since their own countries and organisations paid their salaries and other expenses; they caused no trouble, for their brief was to give of their brains and never of their lips; and they recaptured native hearts by smiling at all times, even when they felt like snarling. They were often confused, disappointed, and frustrated like everyone else, but unlike everyone else they took their tribulations stoically, bearing their Christian cross with Buddhist calm. Those who could not so endure either left in a hurry and were promptly replaced, or did nothing but count the days until they shook the dust of Tiko from their feet.

Overall, the arrangement was cushily convenient for everyone concerned; aliens had their opportunity to atone for the past joys of their compatriots and to woo natives away from the balalaika; Tiko maintained uninterrupted essential services at piddling financial cost, enabling her to cleanse herself of those who had lost their essential indigenous personality. Moreover both parties put up with each other for short periods only, since most foreigners left after two or at most three years, departing just before they went around the bend, or knew too much, or were in a position to do real harm—or real good.

And as clouds flew over the bridge and much water passed under it things began to return to the good old days when no one worried about bears or had heard of localisation. And with it came a different type of expatriate, including an increasing number of old colonial hands. These latecomers and returnees felt no guilt for anyone's sin, didn't give a damn about fickle affections, refused to go around the bend, and knew too much for anyone's good, as Sailosi Atiu discovered to his profound personal regret.

After the departure of his first two deputy directors, Sailosi recruited a third, whom he thought was schooled in the approved manner. The deputy had been to a university in South India where he had obtained the degrees of BA, MA, and PhD, all in two and a half years, specialising, some said, in Transcendental Meditation. He was certainly correctly tutored but was not quite with it and, according to his chagrined superior, was less than luminous and more than a little dense. He had also adopted the Indian habit of incessant talk and pointless argumentation. And Sailosi deftly manoeuvred his exit to Australia where he now contributes brilliantly toward that country's development. The fourth deputy, selected on the strength of his religious fervour and sincere demeanour, was dismissed and sentenced to hard labour and enforced chastity for embezzling the Bureau's petty cash and gobbling the forbidden fruits of his director's secretary.

Having looked in vain for a suitable candidate for the deputy's post, Sailosi resorted at last to seeking foreign technical assistance. The day after lodging his application with the Thinking Office he left on six-months' overseas leave, and returned to find someone at the deputy's desk a few feet behind his own.

'Welcome back, sir. How are you? Goodness me, you do look smashing,' greeted the smiling, familiar face.

'What on earth are you doing here, Mr Hobsworth-Smith?' Sailosi exclaimed after a minute of shocked incredulity. He noticed that his former superior had shaved his handle-bar moustache, softened his stiff upper lip somewhat, and donned the Tikong national dress instead of his standard safari shirt, Bengali shorts, and knee-length socks.

'Call me Eric, sir,' Eric returned with an endearing grin that sent goose pimples all the way up from below Sailosi's belt to the base of his skull. 'I've been here three months as your deputy and technical adviser, er . . . sir. Is there anything wrong? Take a seat sir, please,' Eric implored with brow-wrinkling concern, rose, and carried a chair to Sailosi who collapsed on it. Eric smiled, sucking his Falcon pipe. Sailosi reached with a shaking hand for his handkerchief, wiped the pouring sweat from his face and neck, mumbled something about feeling not quite well after a long flight from Los Angeles, and left.

As soon as he got outside the building he dashed two hundred yards to a public telephone, dialled a number, waited, and screamed, 'Who sent that bastard to me?'

'What bastard? ... Oh, I see. You asked for technical assistance and the British sent him,' replied the Chief Thinking Officer.

'But I did not ask for him; I would never in a million years!' shouted Sailosi. 'He's a totally unredeemed running dog.'

'You've got him. Besides, he's a reformed running dog. Didn't you see his smile?'

'Damn his smile! He's not reformed. Listen, he's a wolf in sheep's clothing. He won't be content to remain a mere adviser. He'll try to run the whole damn show again and that's the truth. Get rid of him for me. Please.'

'We can't do that. We can't afford to pay compensation if we break the agreement. Take it easy, he's here for three years only. You could do to him what Hiti did to Mr Higginbotham.'

'You're joking! Mr Higginbotham knew sweet damn all about Tiko; and he had a conscience. This creep knows Tiko too much and he's got no conscience. He's a crook, I tell you!'

'Aren't we all?'

'Fuck you!' Sailosi spat into the mouthpiece, slammed down the telephone, and strode home oblivious to anything and anyone he ploughed through.

Next morning he hastened to the office to be there before anyone else. As he closed the door behind him a sugary voice wormed its way into his consciousness. 'Good morning, good morning to you, sir. Dear, oh dear, you look rather whacked. Go home and take it easy; I'll look after the office for you, sir.'

'I'm quite all right and I can very well look after myself thank you, Mr Hobsworth-Smith.'

'I'm sure you can. Do call me Eric, will you, sir?' implored Eric with a humility and sincerity that finished the day for Sailosi who broke down and wept uncontrollably, said something about missing a beloved daughter he had left in Los Angeles, pushed himself from his chair, and found his way home a crushed man. Eric smiled and puffed his Falcon pipe. This went on for a few more days until Eric was able to persuade Sailosi not to bother coming to the office at all. Every day a clerk takes correspondence and files to the Director's house. Sailosi telephones instructions to the clerk who relays them to Eric who acts on them as he sees fit.

It's been like this for the last twenty-four months and Sailosi has done little besides count the days until his deputy's departure. The Englishman on the other hand has used his time astutely, grabbing every opportunity to display his streamlined efficiency and to invite the appropriate people to his lavish dinner parties. And unbeknownst to Sailosi Atiu, Eric Hobsworth-Smith has received assurances from the powers-that-be that at the end of his present contract he will be given another three-year term with an option on further renewal.

'Welcome to Tiko!' Manu sang out one day when he saw someone trying to sell a tiki to Eric, whom he had taken for a tourist.

The Big Bullshit

Unlike most of his fellow villagers Pulu has ceased praying and going to church although he is neither an atheist nor an agnostic. He has not forgiven the Lord whom he blames for the troubles he recently had with the three cows and the bull he acquired as aid from New Zealand. Pulu had set out to build from this small beginning a herd that would make him the most prosperous man in Saisaipē.

Before he became a grazier Pulu had raised neither a cow nor a bull, although he had accumulated considerable experience in handling lesser creatures of which stunted pigs were the largest. His love for small animals dates from his childhood when he persistently raised cats and dogs despite their constant disappearance into other people's pots and pans.

Pulu's fondness for animals matches his aversion to plants. He nevertheless confines this sentiment to gardening only, for he harbours no objection whatever to eating yam, sweet potato, or banana, provided always that he doesn't have to grow them. Those who know him well say that his aversion to horticulture is a result of secondary schooling. When he was twelve Pulu parted from his cats and dogs and enrolled at Potopoto College to study mathematics, science, and English so he could enter university and become a veterinarian. Instead he found himself spending half his time cultivating cassava patches for the school food supply, since Potopoto lacked funds and had to compel Pulu and four hundred other boarders to grow cassava. For the rest of the time Pulu was too tired to learn anything.

It came as no surprise when, midway through his second year at the college, Pulu gave up and went home to his father and mother, vowing never to return to school and never to grow another cassava or any other plant. Consequently, for twenty years he did nothing but raise cats, dogs, chickens, and pigs around his house. But since he had no gardens his animals largely fended for themselves, growing runty and wily and therefore safe from theft. This enabled Pulu to amass for himself the largest collection of scrawny small animals in the whole of Saisaipē.

During one of his frequent inspections of his flock Pulu overheard two neighbourhood ladies talking.

'Yes, Ohule's just returned from Tulisi.'

'What was he doing there?'

'Well, it's the craziest thing, you know. He went to try his luck. He said that if he fooled those kids at the Ministry of Agriculture we'd have a whole cow for dinner on Christmas day.'

'And how was he going to do it?'

'Promise you'll keep it to yourself.'

'You know me; I won't say anything to anyone.'

'I know you only too well; and if you let this out I'll tear you to bits. Well, it's like this, you see. Last night, as I was on my way home from a choir practice at the Church Hall I took the short cut over there and happened to walk by the Taulevas' bedroom window. You know me, I don't eavesdrop; it's disgusting and it's against the rules of the School of Angels; but as I got to the bedroom window I couldn't help hearing this awful noise. It was so awful, and it sidetracked me so much that I bumped my head against the window ledge. You can imagine the pain! I stopped to rub my poor head and the terrible noise went on and on and got louder and louder, and I was so worried about it that the pain went away, just like that! But the noise never stopped, and do you know what it was? Well, you know me, I hate to gossip, God be my witness, I really do, but old Sapele and Soana were at it again, and making so much noise! Every time I go past that window they are at it, again and again, and at their age too! Can you imagine! And though my headache had gone I was still groggy so I leaned on the window ledge to keep my balance and, by accident, my eyes were right at the gap between the curtains, and the things I saw were so disgusting, so utterly disgusting! And they had the radio on but it couldn't drown out the noise, and Sapele's mind was only half on the job for he was counting back from 1000—he was counting out aloud for goodness' sake! He had told Soana before, I heard it right outside that very same window some time ago, he told her that he did it so that he could stay longer to please her, can you imagine! Anyway, when Soana was just about to get to the top, judging by the racket she was making, Sapele suddenly stopped and sat up, just like that for goodness' sake! And I saw it accidentally with my own two eyes! And was Soana cross! I was cross too, I really was! Anyway, Soana jumped up and hit him and hit him and I'd have hit him too, I was so cross! And he begged her to stop because he'd done it on purpose, he'd done it on purpose for goodness' sake! And that truly floored Soana, and it nearly did me too, it almost did. I was so furious! And Soana was so livid she fell down and cried and cried, and I cried too, and do you know what that slob said while we were crying? He had the gall to ask her whether she'd heard the announcement on the radio, that's what the slob said for goodness' sake! I was so furious! And Soana was so furious that she got up and rushed out to go to her mum's for good, and I ducked under the house and got my head bumped once more, my poor head! And just before she got to the road Soana realised that she had nothing on, not a single stitch on for goodness' sake! So she rushed back in and that broke them up and they laughed and laughed, and I almost did too. I almost did! So I swallowed my arm to keep from laughing and before I knew it they were at it again, at it again for goodness' sake! And Soana was so relieved and happy and I was so relieved and happy too, I really was! And afterwards when we'd got our breath back, he told her that when he had counted down to 600, and that's a bloody lie, he could never last that long, you can take it from me as I've seen them accidentally so often before; anyway, he said that when he got down to 600 he heard it announced that if any-one was interested in starting a herd of cattle he should con-tact the Ministry of Education, I mean the Ministry of

Agriculture. Sapele was most interested and that's what stopped him in his tracks like I said. Then he told Soana that he was going to town in the morning to try to get a cow from the Ministry for their daughter's wedding next month. Anyway, by then I felt much better. I no longer felt groggy, and as I hate eavesdropping, I really do, I made my way home and told Ohule all about it, but he was not at all interested in Sapele's sex life, can you imagine! All that useless man said to me was, Good, we'll have a whole cow for Christmas! Then this morning he upped and announced that he was going to town to con those kids at the Ministry, like I said, and off he went.'

'How come those kids got cows to give away?'

'He said the cows came from New Zealand aid. Seems like the Kiwis are trying to turn Tiko into a regular pastureland by providing anyone interested with a small beginning for a bigger end. Well Ohule certainly needs a bigger end than the one he's got, but you know what? All he's interested in is food for Christmas and that's six months away for goodness' sake!'

'And what happened in Tulisi? Did he get anything?'

'Did he not; it's the craziest thing. He got back with not one but two for goodness' sake! A bloody cow and a bloody bull and he said he's not interested in big ends. He's out there this very moment fattening the beasties for Christmas. Lord help me, I won't have a chance with him till next year for Chrissake!'

Pulu was most impressed with what he had heard. He was not in the least interested in Sapele's conjugal ups and downs, nor in food for Christmas, but in small beginnings and bigger ends. So next day he went to Tulisi and obtained without cost to himself three cows and a bull, with four chains and collars for tethering them to coconut trees.

On the first night Pulu bowed his head and thanked God for the people of New Zealand, asking Him to keep them generous and to make him, Pulu B. Makau, the biggest cattleman in Saisaipē and beyond. And, as he thought of his herd, his hopes soared as high as an old coconut tree. So far he had raised only small animals, with smashing success, since none had gone astray to return no more. Now he was moving as ordained by the Lord to bigger things in life with beasts much larger than those he had hitherto handled.

But on the second night Pulu's fattest and friendliest cow vanished, collar, chain, and all, never to be seen again. He searched and prayed to the Almighty for the return of his cow, but to no avail. At the same time, he noticed certain people in Saisaipē walking around with strange smiles on their faces and carrying tummies that bulged even more than they normally did. He suspected the worst, and became most frustrated since he could do nothing without evidence.

During the weeks that followed Pulu assigned his children each to sleep at night with a cow or the bull to protect them from the forces of evil. And as the beasts grew bigger and rounder his hopes for the heights revived.

Then one stormy evening his eldest son, returning from the bush with a bunch of bananas he had filched from a neighbour's garden, expired when struck by a bolt of lightning.

Saisaipē turned out in a body for the funeral, expecting a feed to follow. Pulu slaughtered all his chickens and pigs, and gave the lot to the village, begging them to disperse since he wished not to consume their valuable time. The villagers took their meat home, only to return to mourn some more. When he saw them reappearing, Pulu counted his blessings, found them short, and wept.

Next morning he borrowed money from his relatives and bought a truckload of bread which he presented to the village, asking them to leave since they had children to scrub and gardens to tend. The mourners ate their bread, showing no inclination whatsoever to leave.

That was when Pulu realised that Saisaipē was after a cow. The very thought made him howl in despair, tearing at his hair and banging his head against the wall. That evening he informed the Almighty that if it be His will that he be parted from yet another cow, as He had willed it on Job in days long since gone, then he, Pulu B. Makau, could not but obey. He waited for a sign, saw a gecko drop from the ceiling, and knew what must be done. Next day he killed a cow and gave it to the mourners, who took their meat and promptly dispersed.

Pulu remained morose for months thereafter. His eldest

61

son, his entire collection of chickens and pigs, and half his development project had come to nothing. He took his remaining cow and the bull and tethered them outside his house, sending his children to the bush for grass to feed them with. And every day he implored the Almighty to inflict no more deaths on his family until he had built up his vanishing herd.

But being a man of practical bent Pulu also resorted to earthly precautions and went to his much neglected grand-father, ninety-three years of age and of late showing signs of departing.

'Is it really you, Pulu?' asked the almost-blind old man.

'Yes, grandpa; it's me all right.'

'What brought you here out of the blue?'

'I came to see how you are.'

'What's your problem? You haven't visited me here for six years. You must be in trouble. Out with it. What do you want?'

'I have no problems, grandpa; I only want to help you.'

'Help me, he says. Why now, when it's too late, Pulu? You haven't done anything for me for as long as I can remember. I don't need your help, grandson; not now and not in the future. I think you came here to see me die.'

'That's the last thing I want, grandpa. Honest to God. All I want is to take you home, to care for you, and to see that you live as long as you wish.'

'Yours has never been a home to me. And I don't wish to live long. I've had enough of this life.'

'Don't say that, grandpa. I want you to live for at least another five years, and preferably more. You see, grandpa, I'm building up this herd and I want you to live and see it when it's really developed. I want you to be proud of your only son's only son.'

'Get this straight, Pulu. I don't want ever to see anything of yours. Please leave me to die peacefully. I shall be gone in a few days.'

'No, grandpa! You must not! If you die now, you won't have much of a funeral. And I'll have to kill my only bull and probably the cow as well. Hang on for five years at least. I promise to kill twelve cows when you go. Then you shall have the biggest and best funeral Saisaipē has ever seen. Oh, no, no. Grandpa? Grandpa! Wake up, grandpa! I'll make it all up to you, I promise, wake up! Don't go yet for the love of God! Please don't do it to me! Oh, my God, what'll happen to my development project?'

And once again Saisaipē turned out in a body for the funeral. By then Pulu had grown wiser and, without praying to anyone, told his cousins to kill the bull. Being only half as bright as he, the cousins misheard the message and shot the cow, which they gave to the mourners, who grabbed their shares and disppeared hastily, crying no more.

Left with a bull, and confronted with the problem of raising a herd without a cow, Pulu went for advice to the Resident New Zealand Livestock Adviser, who was tinkering in the cabin of his yacht.

'Wait out there, please. I'll be with you in a sec,' came the friendly voice from the cabin. An hour later the expert emerged, half-soaked and smeared all over with grease. 'Sorry, I had to fix a leak in there before it got out of hand. What can I do for you?'

'I have a problem, sir.'

'You have a problem. I have a problem. Everyone has problems. If there weren't any I wouldn't be in this country, would I? Sorry; what's your specific problem?'

'It's like this, sir. I want to start a herd of cattle, the biggest in our village, but all I have is a bull. Can you help me?'

'How could anyone start anything that way? It's like putting the cart before the horse. But I suppose I'm here to make the impossible happen. That's what experts are for. So, your situation is this. You have a bull but no cows and you want lots of calves. Is that right? Christ, I don't think I can handle that one. Bulls don't give virgin births, you know. Are you sure you're in your right mind? Sorry, I didn't mean to offend; it's that this is the best one I've come across in years.' The expert paused for a while, shaking his head as if he was trying to get something out of his ear. 'Yes, I think it's coming now. Well, is your bull's manhood complete and intact?'

'I don't quite get you, sir.'

'Oh, I see. Let's put it another way. Is your bull well hung? You still don't get it, eh? Well then, let me ask a less complicated one. Where the hell did you get that bloody bull from?'

'Sir, it came from New Zealand.'

'Good Lord, why didn't you say so at the beginning? That bull's one hundred per cent complete, intact, and well hung! New Zealand never sends duds abroad. I bet you ten dollars that that lovely Kiwi stud can screw every single Tikong bitch in a single day, no sweat. Your problems are over, Pulu. Cheer up and listen carefully to some expert advice. The position is this. There are many cows in Tiko, right? and there aren't many bulls here, right? Well, let's hope so for your own sake. Now, suppose you hire out your bull to service other people's cows in return for one calf in every two, what would you get?'

'A three-year sentence for pimping, sir.'

'Pimping my foot! We're dealing here with decent, dumb animals and not with some overdone hookers. And it's standard practice in every great Christian nation, God's Own Country included. If you really want to raise the biggest herd with only a bull, that's the only way you can do it. If you reject my advice you'd better forget about your development project or try getting your bull to give virgin births. I believe the Australian vet could help you with that one.'

Pulu went home, thought about it, and decided reluctantly to take the New Zealander's advice. Accordingly he led his bull from village to village looking for cows to service. He soon discovered the task to be much more difficult than he had imagined, for everyone he approached who had cows also had a bull or two, needing no extra care. He persisted regardless and, as it was bound to happen sooner or later, landed on someone with a cow and no bull. The owner was an elderly priest who had preached for fifty years against sins of all denominations, in particular against those of the flesh, which he deemed disgusting beyond salvation. His flock told Pulu that although he had kept the animal for three years, there had been no calf. Pulu saw his opportunity for making a deal with the holy man and his cow.

Thus, followed by his bull, he presented himself to the priest who was sitting on the veranda of his house.

'God's blessings upon you, my son,' said the priest piously after Pulu had sat down on a cane chair beside him. 'What brought you to this far-away place?'

'I have come to see you, father, and I have brought Nailavo along.'

'Nailavo? Who is Nailavo, if I may ask?'

'That's him over there, father; the bull.'

'I see. He's certainly a handsome creature; and you have brought him along to me?'

'Yes, father.'

'Bless you a thousand times, my son. And thank you very, very much for your generosity. Praise be to God. He has answered my prayers as He has done many, many times before. You see, we are building a new clinic but we are running into some financial difficulties. We need another $400 for the ceiling which we must have. I prayed long last night beseeching the Heavenly Father to help us with our problem. Today He has sent you to give me that beautiful beast which will fetch just the amount we need. We're most. . . .'

'Ahem, father. I'm sincerely sorry, but it's not quite like that. You see, Nailavo's in business. He and I would like to help you out, but it will have to be on a long-term basis. You have that lovely, sweet cow over there, father. You need calves, and when those calves grow up, you can have as many ceilings as you like. But before you have calves you must have a cow and a bull at the very least. I know it's difficult for you to understand, father, seeing as how you've never married and experienced what it means but, father, I must come to the point at once. You see, Nailavo would like to make friends with your sweet and lovely cow, you know what I mean. He's a New Zealander from a good stock and is very strong and, according to the Resident New Zealand Livestock Adviser, he can, in a single day, screw every bitch. . . .'

But Pulu didn't finish his sentence, for the priest went berserk, slapped him on the face with surprising energy for one so old, and threw him out of his house.

'No!' he screamed at the fast retreating figures of Pulu and his bull. 'My cow's a virgin and will commit no sin as long as I live!'

Though shaken and dismayed Pulu determined to continue with his quest. He pressed on relentlessly until one day he happened upon Manu tending a cow for a friend, one Aleki Lahi, government clerk class two, who had assumed grazing as a sideline more promising of greater things than his current occupation.

'How are you, my friend?' Manu called out.

'I'm in trouble, and the Lord has abandoned me,' Pulu sighed, sitting down to unburden his heart, after which Manu told him of Aleki's misadventures with his cattle.

It turned out that Aleki had received a small beginning for a bigger end from the Australian Aid Scheme for the Pacific Islands. And for reasons known only to themselves the Australians had sent him three bulls and a cow for a start. Within two months, however, one bull that had grown too big for his collar had, while dreaming of his native land where he had roamed untethered, strangled himself trying to break loose from his chain. Another went for a feast for the opening of a new church in which Aleki was the door-keeper and collector of tithes, dues, and other forms of holy extortion. Soon after, the high chief of his district visited him, pointed a finger at the remaining bull, and proclaimed, 'That beast will be mine when properly fattened.' Aleki's heart sank but, being raised to obey his betters, and being obliged to the chief for his government post, he collected himself, castrated the bull, and fattened it for when required. Thus Aleki was left with a cow—and a bull with no balls, of no use whatever for service.

Following the tales of woe, Manu, who hates the kinds of development taking place in Tiko, pitied his friends so much that he temporarily shelved his aversion and succeeded in urging Aleki to put his cow in a pen with Pulu's bull for mutual comfort and multiplication. But something unforseen occurred: for no apparent reason the cow turned wild and bitchy, allowing no one to go near her; and, equally inexplicably, the bull limped to a corner and sat tight, looking confused and embarrassed.

This was awful, said Pulu, who once again consulted the Resident New Zealand Livestock Adviser. The great expert examined the beasts thoroughly, scratched his head and exclaimed, 'My God, that stupid Australian cow's a lesbian!'

'What's a lesbian, sir?' asked Aleki, having never heard the word before.

'Never mind; it's best you don't know,' the New Zealander replied. Not being satisfied, Aleki appealed to a visiting veterinarian touring Tiko with an Australian Parliamentary Delegation as their physician. The doctor examined the beasts from head to tail, poked here and poked there, monitored their behaviour for two days and two nights, grabbed Pulu's arm and said, 'You won't believe this, mate, but that bloody New Zealand bull's impotent.'

'What's impotent, sir?'

'Jeeze. Don't bother; it's not important,' the Australian replied and walked away.

But Manu, who had noted the experts' esoteric words, consulted the dictionary, grinned from ear to ear, then roared with delight. For many years he had preached against development but no one had bothered to listen. Certain this time that he had turned the corner, Manu hopped on his bicycle and pedalled all over the island carrying a placard that read:

DEVELOPMENT IS A LIE
TIKO KNOWS SWEET BUGGER ALL
AUSTRALIAN COWS ARE QUEER
AND NEW ZEALAND BULLS CAN'T DO NO DAMN
GOOD EITHER

He succeeded with at least two men. Aleki Lahi abandoned his hope for riches from cattle, resigning himself to living on his meagre government salary. Pulu B. Makau sold his bull and with the proceeds bought chickens and pigs to launch the beginning of another biggest collection of scrawny small animals in the whole of Saisaipē. And both men swore never again to pray for help or to take any more bullshit from Tiko, Australia, or New Zealand.

Blessed are the Meek

It is said that an American likes to walk tall even though he may be short, and that he occasionally takes a giant step or two for mankind even though mankind may not have asked him to. Good luck to him, says Manu, and may he live long, what with the energy crisis, rising unemployment, falling Skylabs, policing human rights, and carrying other heavy global responsibilities befitting a member of the Greatest Nation on Earth.

A Tikong, on the other hand, tends to walk short even though he may be tall, and will not take even a dwarfish step if he can help it. He normally lives too long on account of his love for energy conservation, which he achieves with enviable success simply by doing as little as possible or by doing nothing at all if he can. He does not have to police human rights, even in his own village, since he's never heard of such things. Moreover, he has no global responsibility, for he is a citizen of a tiny country, so small that mankind is advised not to look for it on a classroom globe for it will only search in vain. More often than not cartographers leave Tiko out of their charts altogether because they can't be bothered looking for a dot sufficiently small to represent it faithfully and at the same time big enough to be seen without the aid of a microscope. So much by way of introduction; now let's return to the point. The point is Puku Leka who is really not a point but a tall man who appears short.

But how can a tall man look diminutive, one may legitimately ask, especially if one has never thought in opposites or never set foot in Tiko where everything is simultaneously possible and impossible. We may demonstrate the point by abstracting some examples from the life-history of Puku Leka, in whose ample person is embodied the nobility characteristic of the humble citizenry of Tiko.

Now forty years of age, Puku came into the world on a rainy day, a twelve-pound baby and last of the three children born to Mr and Mrs Tuki Leka who adhered faithfully to the Old Testament dictum that one regularly beats the object of one's affection. Mr and Mrs Leka led a life of bliss and contentment, a happy connubial state brought about by Mr Leka's acumen and wisdom. At the beginning of their married life Mrs Leka was an extremely pretty, vivacious, wilful, and outspoken girl. Within three years Mr Leka had flattened and ironed out the vivacity, the wilfulness, and the outspokenness simply by slapping and belting Mrs Leka whenever she spoke out or did anything displeasing to him.

Even in old age Mrs Leka was still beautiful, but she had become a soft-spoken, sedate lady who obeyed, respected, and loved her husband. She often joked about how Mr Leka used to beat the living daylights out of her, and of her beloved's other just visitations. And Mr Leka would smile patriarchally, secure in the knowledge of a job exemplarily done. In later life Mr Leka beat Mrs Leka only occasionally, about once every three months: a sharp jab here and a quick kick there, mild, affectionate reminders of who's boss.

As for Puku, he was a most fortunate child in having an elder brother and an elder sister in addition to his mum and dad to slap him into shape and to wring and squeeze him into the approved mould, always with loving rage. If he spoke out of turn, as when he dared ask for more at meal times, or if in frustration he unwittingly uttered an unseemly word, he was sharply reprimanded or, more often, slashed into silence. If he rose when he should sit tight, he was slammed down hard and a dart of pain would shoot up from his bottom through the spine to the base of his skull, sending appropriate messages of goodness into his brain. When he sneaked away and played too long with other children, or when he took two hours to deliver a message that should have taken him only five minutes, he was set to run ten times around the yard, contributing to his physical growth and fitness.

His charming sister had a favourite and effectively benefi-cial way of moulding him. When he teased her, or more com-monly whenever she felt like it, she would grab his left ear, twisting and pulling it upward, and he would strain his head, stand on his toes, and crease his face in delicious agony. As a result, his left ear grew twice the size of the other, vastly improving his aural capacity.

His father reminded him daily of what Jehovah did to those who pleased Him and to those who stirred His wrath. Although Puku was pleased with the idea of Heavenly rewards, it was the notion of the Lord's punishment that remained so vivid in his mind. He had little dreams of his being quartered and fed bit by bit into the Eternal Fire, and he would scream and shout promises of remaining for ever pure. He developed a healthy respect for the Lord.

In addition to his conditioning through thumping and threat of Eternal Roast, Puku received excellent training in bowing and bending and crawling. Whenever he walked into a gathering of adults he bent his body and bowed his head as he stepped gingerly to wherever he was instructed to pro-ceed. At the twice-daily family prayers he knelt and bent his torso so that his head rested on the floor in the manner of infidels on their prayer rugs; and as prayers in Tiko were usually conducted at greater length than just about anywhere else, Puku would thus bow to the Almighty for upward of half an hour each time, and much longer when he went to church. He also spent much time crouching behind low bushes and other objects, concealing himself from his lov-ingly wrathful family.

And Puku did a lot of crawling. When the high chief of his district visited his father's house, or when Puku was dis-patched to the high chief, he would drop on all fours and creep to him with proper respect and self-abasement. When he went to see important persons, he crawled in their pres-ence, often dragging behind him some heavy gifts, a practice much encouraged by his family as the only effective way peo-ple of his like could get things to move in their direction.

Thus by the time he had grown into a six-foot-four-inch man, Puku had become so accustomed to bowing, bending, and crawling that he could not sit, stand, or walk straight.

These were not the only factors in Puku's deceptive physical appearance; far from it. At primary school he was an object of joy and mirth for he was such a meek, mild, and awkward child. Much shorter boys than he, who strutted like tall cocks, jumped on his back or jabbed his stomach to see him fall to his knees. And everyone laughed at him, including his teachers. Puku took it all stoically, always praying to God to grant him greater endurance and to enable him to bear his cross with Christian fortitude.

And because he was told that he wasn't bright Puku believed that he was mentally backward and did much worse in his examinations than his native ability would have warranted. He nevertheless qualified for Potopoto College, where he spent much of his time crouching over low desks. He began showing interest in his school work and surprised himself and everyone else by performing very well in his examinations.

But just as he started to shine, hard times descended on Tiko when copra prices plummeted. As his father could not afford to keep all his children at school, Puku, the youngest, though brightest, left Potopoto College to spend the following decades on his father's land as a full-time subsistence farmer, an occupation that was much lauded by leaders everywhere but which earned him neither sufficient money nor standing nor the affection of women.

His brother and sister completed their schooling, secured lucrative employment, married partners with good connections, and got loans from the Bank of Tiko to build concrete houses for themselves. Puku, on the other hand, built on a corner of his father's land a traditional thatched house that was traditionally small, traditionally dark, and traditionally damp, a traditionally appropriate abode for a man of his lowly station. Inside the house Puku kept traditional company with rats, cockroaches, bugs of every description, and a thousand other tiny creatures of the Lord's creation.

Then his father died. And the land on which Puku lived and worked went by right of primogenital inheritance to his elder brother who lived in town, never worked on it, and had no intention of working on it. The brother also leased out to a wealthy farmer all of it except that tiny corner on which Puku's hut stood. And, by the same primogenital right, the elder brother also inherited everything else from their father. Although Puku was left with nothing, he accepted his lot and accepted also the notion that one day he would be rewarded with an estate in Heaven.

When his brother leased out the land Puku was forced to apply for a daily-paid unskilled labourer's job with a government department. He was summoned for an interview presided over by the departmental head. It turned out that he was the only interviewee for the job, but he didn't know that until much later.

'Why did you apply for this position?' asked the departmental head.

'I need the job very urgently, sir.'

'Why?'

'I have no means of support, sir.'

'Have you applied for a job before?'

'No, sir.'

'Why not?'

'I never had the need to, sir.'

'What educational qualifications have you got?'

'I have no certificate, sir. I did well at college but I didn't finish.'

'Good. You're the only applicant without a certificate of any kind. It's been to your advantage. The job's yours. And you'll get eight dollars a week. What work have you done before?'

'I've been gardening for twenty-five years, sir.'

'Why did you give it up?'

'My elder brother inherited my father's land and leased it out.'

'Are you a good gardener?'

'Yes, sir. And I love it, sir.'

'Very good. So you have a skill to fall back on if anything happens. Excellent. You don't need to work your way up to an established position then. You can be laid off any time. You're lucky you have another skill.'

'But I have no land, sir.'

'It doesn't matter. As long as you have a back-up skill God will always find something for you to do. We're not concerned with those whom the Almighty looks after. After all, He's a much greater provider than all of us put together. Do you have your own house?'

'Sort of, sir....'

'But a house nevertheless....'

'Sir, it's not really a decent....'

'As long as we have our own roofs over our own heads, everything's fine. Thank God we're not in Bangladesh. Anyway, you're fortunate to have a house of your own. More so than most senior government officials. The state has to provide for us poor sods.'

'You mean with those huge houses all over the town, sir?'

'Yes. But to go back to your case. Since you have your own house you don't need a pension. The state can't afford to give everyone a pension; only some, like those who have no houses of their own. You look strong and healthy.'

'The Lord's been kind to me, sir.'

'Obviously. Let's hope that He'll always be kind to you. You're too strong and too healthy to qualify for sick or annual leave or any of that sort of nonsense. Leave is only for the weak and the unhealthy. That's all for now, Puku. Welcome to your new responsibility; I hope you'll do your best for Tiko. Report for work at eight-thirty sharp tomorrow.'

Although he was troubled by the conditions of his employment, Puku took the job. He had no choice. And, like so many lowly people with problems they couldn't solve themselves, he sought out Manu, who advised him to leave the job. But since he insisted on keeping it, Manu told him that if that was the case he shouldn't think about working conditions. It wouldn't do him any good, especially in view of the fact that Tiko has no such things as unions.

'My friend,' Manu concluded, 'in this less than just world of ours, only those who have coronary conditions and who suffer from obesity, diabetes, high blood pressure, chronic diarrhoea, gout, and other afflictions of affluence, are entitled to highly paid, secure jobs with superannuation, and sick and

73

annual leave, in addition to other fringe benefits, for they will neither live long on earth nor will they inherit anything in Heaven. Ultimately, Puku, one must feel sorry for the poor sods. And that's my final advice to you: be sorry for them and not for yourself. That way, you'll feel a little better in this worst of all possible worlds.'

And so today Puku still works diligently as the cleaner for the same government department. He spends his spare time doing chores for his brother and sister who so use him on the grounds that since he has neither a wife nor children he must help those laden with family responsibilities. His pastor requires him to contribute generously to the Church, and his neighbourhood expects him to give of his time and energy to communal undertakings. He gives and gives in return for which he receives words: of appreciation and love, of pious blessings and encouragement to continue suffering through life as Christ did so long ago and, best of all, of assurances of eternal rewards in Life Hereafter.

In the judgement of his people Puku Leka is a good man and a noble example of what a Tikong should be. He knows his standing in his community and pays proper respect to his earthly betters; he is patient, long suffering, and devoid of personal ambition; he carries the burden for his family, church, village, and country without complaint and without much expectation of earthly reward. He and countless others of his kind are essential for the continued stability of the realm of Tiko. And although he is a tall man he walks short, for his spirit is humbled and his back permanently bent.

Bopeep's Bells

His Holiness Bopeep Dr Toki Tumu comes from Chamber Island which, like many other places in the South Pacific, received its refined designation from the venerable Captain James Cook, who was given to naming the places he discovered as a way of honouring friends and patrons, or in commemoration of salient events. Chamber Island was so named to record for posterity the occasion when some of its inhabitants relieved the great navigator of his much loved and much sat-upon chamber pot. When, after a futile search for the missing vessel, the bereft Captain Cook set sail for New Zealand, the then chief of the island confiscated the stolen item and declared it his special kava drinking bowl. Ten years later, when the chief had taken to imbibing sailors' rum straight from the bottle and had eschewed drinking impotent kava, he gave the pot to his concubines to use for brewing tea for the island's first white missionary who, upon discovering how his beverage had been prepared, left his post in an unchristian huff, proclaiming that the next cup of tea he drank would be in Heaven.

Toki Tumu is a descendent of one of the thieves of Captain Cook's chamber pot. He had arrived in the world on a Sunday morning when church bells had just begun booming the call for the dawn service. This deafening initial experience so indelibly stamped itself into his infant brain that Toki grew up obsessed with bells. The first toy he asked for from his parents was a bell, and indeed the only toys he ever wanted and played with were bells. By the time he turned forty he could ring two hundred and fifty different rhythms with the bells he had hanging outside his house.

Toki had pigs, goats, chickens, and ducks running around the yard. To summon them he employed a series of different bell rings, not only for each animal species but for the particular purposes for which they were called. When the pigs heard the bell ring for a feed, they hastened home from wherever they were to receive their daily bread; and so did the goats, the chooks, and the ducks. Toki was so adept at conditioning through bells that he could, with a special ring, summon an animal to come obediently to be slaughtered.

One Sunday morning, while still under the influence as a result of an all-night beer party, Toki, for the first time and without intending to, gave the distinctive rhythmic ring of church bells calling the faithful to their Houses of Worship. It was the best and the most beautiful ring that that particular rhythm had ever been given. And it was magnetic in its effect, for to his utter amazement Toki saw the entire population of the island making its way toward his house. As they came they sang hymns, confessed their sins publicly, praised the Lord, and prayed with passion abandoned.

It soon dawned upon Toki that like his little animals his fellow islanders were thoroughly conditioned by church bells summoning them for their spiritual sustenance. When they had all gathered around his house Toki did not know what to do so he continued ringing the bell and the people went on singing, confessing, and praying. Three hours later Toki collapsed in a heap and the gathering ceased what they were doing and dispersed quietly, thoroughly drained by their spiritual outpouring.

That incident took Toki into alley-ways of thought that led eventually to a fateful idea which he tested by ringing the same rhythmic sound at different times of day and night. And, to confirm his hunch, the entire island population turned up regularly and piously. Seeing the hand of Providence at work Toki began preaching to the assembled multitude. Again, to his surprise, he discovered that he possessed considerable oratorical ability; the congregation responded to every word he uttered with cries of Amen, Hallelujah, and Hosannah. When he finally invited them to confess their sins they rose in a body and revealed their innermost thoughts and their most private deeds. And when he called upon them to give their lives to the Saviour they filed up enthusiastically to be blessed. But when he appealed to them to donate money for the Lord's work they balked and went home shaking their heads.

Toki resolved to overcome the problem, for the success of his aim to become the premier fund-raiser for the Lord, and incidentally for himself, depended upon his ability to persuade people to dip into their pockets. He prayed, meditated, received an inspiration, wrote down a new bell tune and practised it in his head until he got it right and ready. One Sunday when the island population had gathered at his place he rang a sound so sweet and sad that everyone wept. And while doing this with one hand, Toki used the other to drop coins into a bucket in such a rhythmic way that the clanking and clinking sound they made added greater poignancy and sadness to the music of the bell. The congregation was so moved that they wailed louder and louder as they shuffled up to the bucket to add their coins. When it was all over, three six-gallon buckets were filled to the brim.

Toki knew then that he was in big business. He assembled a fund-raising group which toured the length and breadth of Tiko with two bells and fifty six-gallon buckets, which were filled within two weeks, so effective were the sounds produced by Toki from his bells, accompanied by the sweet clanking and clinking of coins. The Bank of Tiko ran out of silver as a result and contacted Toki for a loan of all that he had at a twenty per cent interest rate payable within a month, which was considerably more generous than the Bank charged its own customers. Toki and his Chamber Island Concert Bells Ensemble made several more smashingly succcessful tours of the realm, after each of which he granted a loan to the coinless Bank of Tiko.

Then one night, while meditating, he had a resounding vision. A bearded man dressed in white robes appeared standing under a gigantic golden bell, pulling at the rope and producing thunderous booms. He paused and, staring unblinkingly at Toki, announced: 'I am commanded by the Almighty Ruler of Heaven and Earth to tell you to establish a New Church. Amen.' Before Toki could respond the celestial messenger had vanished, and so had the golden bell.

Toki was very flattered by his being specifically selected over all others for the sacred task. More importantly, he saw in his mandate a heaven-sent opportunity to raise more funds, to become a leader, and to be famous. He had always known that organised religion was the most effective instrument, in Tiko at least, for the attainment of wealth, power, and renown.

So Toki set about organising an Institution using the existing structures of churches in Tiko and elsewhere as his guide. First, a Church must have a Name. Toki prayed, meditated, had a revelation, and rang his bell. When everyone had assembled he proclaimed: 'I am commanded by the Almighty Ruler of Heaven and Earth to establish a new religion the name of which shall, forevermore, be the Church of the Golden Bell. Amen.' He gave a ding, a dong, and a dell in rapid succession and the congregation chorused its Amen and dispersed.

Next, the New Church must have a Leader with Impressive Titles. Toki went to sea and fasted for seven days and seven nights, after which he felt such an overwhelming sense of power that he stepped off his dinghy to walk on the water and almost drowned. He cast a quick look around and praised the Lord that no one had seen him splashing in the brine.

Upon his return he rang the bell and in front of the whole assembly appointed himself Leader, with the titles of Bishop, President, Prophet, and Doctor. The title 'Bishop' stood for his holy appointment and sartorial beauty, 'President' for his fund-raising and organisational ability, and 'Prophet' for the things by which he would be remembered. He awarded himself the Degree of Doctor of Righteousness for the number of times he had read the entire Bible, for the great length of his prayers and sermons, and for the frequency of feasts given in his honour.

Since it was awkward to refer to him as His Holiness Bishop, President, and Prophet Dr Toki Tumu, he announced that he should be addressed simply as His Holiness Bopeep Dr Tumu. He was thrilled by the sound of his combined titles, for Bopeep was very close to Beepee, the famous South Pacific word that meant godliness in commerce.

Next, a Church must have a Constitution. Toki sat in a puddle for ten days and ten nights, and through prayer and meditation arrived at the conclusion that all existing Church Constitutions were No Good. He looked outside religion for a model and discovered that the best charter in history had been the British Constitution. He left the puddle, scraped the mud off himself, rang the bell with a ding, a dong, and a dang in slow motion and announced to the multitude: 'I am commanded by the Almighty Maker of Laws that bind Heaven and Earth to declare to you and to all that our Constitution shall, forevermore, remain Unwritten. Being so, our beloved Constitution needs no explanation whatsoever. Any Church member who wishes to know the contents of the Constitution needs only to pray and reflect and they shall be revealed to him or to her in all their Glory. For our Constitution is stamped in the Soul of the Congregation and in the Head of His Holiness the Bopeep. And since the Soul's only concern is in matters Heavenly and Saintly, it lies entirely on the Head of the Bopeep and on no one else's to interpret our Constitution, and only when absolutely necessary. Amen.'

Next, Toki climbed to the top of the tallest coconut tree, where he fasted for twelve days and twelve nights after which he was so filled with a sense of omnipotence that he was just about to take off on a flight to demonstrate his power when wiser counsel prevailed. So he climbed slowly down like a mere mortal and went home.

Then he rang the bell and proclaimed the Nature and Extent of the Constitutional Powers vested in the Office of the Bopeep. 'Our Constitution is based on the Doctrine of the Infallibility of the Bopeep. This being so, His Holiness can do no wrong, can think no evil, and can tell no lies. His Holiness is, therefore, incorruptible. Thus endowed with Divine Perfection the Bopeep can do anything he wants, for his decisions and actions are spotless in the eyes of the Lord. It also follows that the Holy Bopeep has the sole say in the Financial Affairs of the Church of the Golden Bell. Moreover,

just as our Constitution is Unwritten, so all financial trans-
actions of the Church shall, unless otherwise decreed by His
Holiness, remain forevermore Unwritten, and be conducted
in accordance with the Will of the Bopeep. There will be no
Finance Committee or any other Committee within the
Church because such groups always indulge in unchristian
bickering and tend to call for earthly justice which, as you all
know, is man-made and therefore wrong and disgusting since
man is so full of vile thoughts and foul deeds. There is One
Eternal Justice and only His Holiness can say what that is,'
proclaimed Toki, pulling the bell rope and producing a short,
sharp crack which ended with such finality that everyone
assented vigorously and went home utterly impressed by his
authority and charisma.

Having disposed of the institutional problems of the new
church, Toki slept for fourteen days and fourteen nights
without prayer or meditation. When he finally left his bed he
rang the bell and proclaimed that it was absolutely unnecessary to make pronouncements on Spiritual Matters since God
moved in Mysterious Ways which could not be regulated by
Constitutions, written or otherwise. 'Our main concern is
with Institutional Matters. Once these are in order, and once
the Church and its Leaders prosper, Spiritual Affairs will
bloom at the Holy Ghost's behest and in His own Good
Time. Amen.'

Next, Toki declared a Day of Tribute to the Church: 'In
nine months' time Caesar will give his all to God.' And so
for nine months the entire population of Chamber Island cut
and dried copra, packed bananas, sold vanilla, and overstayed
in New Zealand and Australia on working holidays to raise
what belonged to Caesar for offering to God. Toki again led
his Chamber Island Concert Bells Ensemble through the
length and breadth of Tiko, ending with one hundred six-
gallon buckets full of coins. Altogether $1 500 000 was col-
lected, presented, blessed, and locked in a big safe in Toki's
house.

The first thing done with the money thus raised was to
construct, not a House of Worship, but a Two-Storey Mansion for the Bopeep: all heads of Churches in Tiko had two-

storey mansions in order to place them close to Heaven and far from Worldly Temptations, to which they were particularly vulnerable. Toki gave a different explanation. He wanted his house to be the earthly symbol of the golden mansions in Heaven awaiting the wretched of the Earth.

Then Toki equipped his house with all the modern conveniences he could get, not all of which he had ordered. Many were sent as gifts, the most notable of which were items donated by the Proprietor of an Adult Shop in Sydney, the First Lady of a Rejuvenation and Revitalisation Centre in Tokyo, who also produced a certain kind of film, and the Godfather of a Gaming Temple in Taipei.

These three beautiful persons had visited the realm on investment study tours, had subsequently established branches of their concerns in Tulisi, and had sent samples of the best products of their industries as gifts to important people including, of course, religious leaders, as a way of recruiting Church support for or acquiescence to their crusade to turn pious Tiko into the South Pacific Haven for Gambling and Prostitution. This conversion was to be effected through ways that would enhance traditional cultural values, protect the environment, and promote religious prosperity.

And, being afflicted with sleeping sickness and a consequent inability to tell heads from tails or frontsides from backsides, the gormless Churches of Tiko switched off their alarm clocks and snored through the beautification of their country. As for Toki, the gifts from Sydney, Tokyo, and Taipei were quite unnecessary, for he was a man of unmatched virtuosity, physical agility, inventiveness, and staying power.

Next, Toki ordered the biggest and fastest limousine from Detroit. 'This great product of the Greatest Nation on Earth, Land of Prayer and Plenty, is the symbol of Angelic Speed. . . . Get off the bloody road, you stupid oaf!' Toki roared as he zoomed down the dusty highway past a wobbly Hash House Harrier.

Finally, taking his cue from benighted Melanesian cargo cult leaders, Toki assembled a harem of the ten loveliest ladies in Chamber Island. He proclaimed his spiritual loathing for fornication but declared it a necessity that he experience the suffering and agony of sin in order to transcend earthly pleasures. 'It's the only way!' he thundered deliciously from the pulpit, utterly transcended by his nocturnal transport.

And so His Holiness Bopeep Dr Toki Tumu of the Church of the Golden Bell forged ahead building the thriving institution that has spread throughout Tiko and may yet overtake the numerical superiority of the older Churches for, as Manu says, it has the bells that ring best those sweetest sounds of all: the music of coins and coition.

The Glorious Pacific Way

'I hear you're collecting oral traditions. Good work. It's about time someone started recording and preserving them before they're lost for ever,' said the nattily dressed Mr Harold Minte in the slightly condescending though friendly tone of a born diplomat, which Mr Minte actually was.

'Thank you, sir,' Ole Pasifikiwei responded shyly. He was not given to shyness, except in the presence of foreigners, and on this sultry evening at a cocktail party held in the verdant gardens of the International Nightlight Hotel, Ole was particularly reticent.

Through the persistent prodding of an inner voice which he had attributed to that of his Maker, Ole had spent much of the spare time from his job as Chief Eradicator of Pests and Weeds collecting oral traditions, initially as a hobby but in time it had developed into a near obsession. He had begun by recording and compiling his own family genealogy and oral history, after which he expanded into those of other families in his village, then neighbouring settlements, and in seven years he had covered a fifth of his island country. He recorded with pens in exercise books, which he piled at a far corner of his house, hoping that one day he would have a machine for typing his material and some filing cabinets for their proper storage. But he had no money for these luxuries, so he kept to his exercise books, taking care of them as best as he could.

His work on oral traditions attracted the approving notice of the Ministry of Environment, Religion, Culture, and Youth (universally dubbed MERCY), a high official of which, who was also an intimate of Ole's, had invited him to the cocktail party to meet the diplomat visiting Tiko on a project identification and funding mission.

'Perhaps you could do with some financial assistance,' Mr Minte suggested.

'That'll help a lot, sir.'

'We have money set aside for the promotion of culture preservation projects in the Pacific. Our aim is to preserve the Pacific Way. We want to help you.'

'Very generous of you sir. When can I have some money?'

'After you've written me a letter asking for assistance.'

'Do I have to? Can't you just send some?'

'Obviously you haven't dealt with us before.'

'No, sir.'

'Things are never quite that simple, you know. We have the money to distribute, but we can't give it away just like that. We want you to ask us first. Tell us what you want; we don't wish to tell you what you should do. My job is to go around informing people that we want to co-operate for their own good, and people should play their part and ask us for help. Do you get me?'

'Yes, sir. But suppose no one asks?'

'That's no problem. Once people know that they can get things from us for nothing, they will ask. And besides, we can always send someone to help them draw up requests. By the way, who's that jolly chap over there?'

'That's His Excellency the Imperial Governor.'

'My God. I have something very important to tell him. I must see him now before he leaves. Come and see me tomorrow morning at ten at the MERCY Building. Think of what I've said and we'll talk about it then. I'm pleased we've met. Good night.'

Shortly afterwards Ole left for home, disturbed and feeling reduced. He had never before asked for anything from a total stranger. If Mr Minte had money to give, as he said he did, why did he not just give it? Why should he, Ole, be required to beg for it? He remembered an incident from his childhood when a bigger boy offered him a mango then demanded that he fall on his knees and beg for it. Hatred for Mr Minte surged in his stomach to be mixed with self-hatred for his own simplicity and for his relutance to ask from a stranger while everyone else seemed to have been doing so without compunction. He needed a typewriter and some filing cabinets, not for himself but for the important work he had set out to do. Yet pride stood in the way. The Good Book says that pride is the curse of man. The Good Book also says, 'Ask and it shall be given unto you.' One should learn to ask for and accept things with grace. But he could not sleep well that night; his heart was torn—it was not easy to ask from a stranger if you weren't practised at it. He must do it nevertheless. There was no other way of acquiring the facilities he needed. Anyway, he supposed as he drifted into sleep, it's like committing sin: once you start it becomes progressively easier.

At ten the following morning Ole entered the MERCY office where Mr Minte was waiting.

'Good morning, Ole. Have you made up your mind about seeking help from us?'

'Yes, sir. I'd like to have a typewriter and some filing cabinets. I'll write you a letter. Thank you.'

'Now, Ole, I'm afraid that's not possible. As I said last night, things aren't so simple. We don't want to tell people what to do with the money we give, but there are things we cannot fund. Take your particular request for instance. My Minister has to report to our parliament on things people do with the money we give. Once politicians see that we've given a typewriter for culture preservation they will start asking embarrassing questions of my Minister. What's a civilised typewriter to do with native cultures? The Opposition will have a field day on that one. Most embarrassing. That won't do . . . .'

'But in my case it has everything to do. . . .'

'You have to ask for something more directly relevant, I'm sorry. Relevance is the key that opens the world,' Mr Minte said, and paused to savour the profundity of his remark before turning on an appearance of astounding generosity.

'Look, we can give you $2000 a year for the next five years to publish a monthly newsletter of your activities. Send us a copy of each issue, O.K.?'

'But I still need a typewriter to produce a newsletter.'

'Try using a MERCY typewriter. You will have to form a committee, you know.'

'A committee? What for? I've been working alone for seven years and no committee has been interested in me.'

'Oh, they will, they will when good money's involved. The point, however, is that we don't give to individuals, only to organisations. You form a group, call it the Oral Traditions Committee or something, which will then write to us for assistance. Do you follow me?' Mr Minte looked at his watch and lifted an eyebrow. 'I'm sorry, I have to go now to talk with the National Women's Association. Don't you know that your women are more forthcoming and efficient than your men? When we tell them—sorry—suggest that they form a committee, they do so immediately. It's a great pleasure handling them. Their organisations have tons of money from us and other helpers. Think about it and come again tomorrow at the same time. See you then.' Mr Minte went out and disappeared into a black official limousine.

Ole remained in the office keeping very still, as was his habit when angry, breathing deeply until he had regained his equanimity. Then he rose and walked slowly to the office of his intimate, the high MERCY official, who sat quietly and listened until Ole had poured out his heart.

'The trouble with you is that you're too moralistic,' Emi Bagarap said thoughtfully. 'You're too proud, Ole.'

'It's no longer a matter of pride, I've seen to that; it's self-respect.'

'Self-respect is a luxury we can't afford; we have no choice but to shelve it for a while. When we're developed, then we will do something about dignity and self-respect . . . .'

'What if we are never developed?'

'We will develop! There's not a speck of doubt about that. You must cultivate the power of positive thinking,' said Emi Bagarap looking wise, experienced, and positive.

'You must keep in mind, Ole, that we're playing international games in which the others have money and we don't. Simple as that. They set the rules and we play along trying to bend them for our benefit.

'Anyway, those on the other side aren't all that strict with their rules either. Take Mr Minte, for instance. He offers to give you $2000 a year for five years and all he wants is for you to form a committee and then the committee writes a letter asking for the funds and produces a newsletter regularly. But he didn't say anything about how the organisation is to be formed or run. See? You can get three or four friends and form a committee with you as chairman and treasurer, and someone else as secretary. Get only those who're neither too interested nor too knowledgeable. That'll give you the freedom to do what needs to be done.

'Again, the letter asking for help will be from the Committee and not from you personally. Your self-respect will not be compromised, not that it really matters, mind you.

'Furthermore, Mr Minte didn't say anything about the size of your newsletter, did he? Well. You can write it in a page or two taking about half an hour each month. And you don't have to write it in English either. And if you so wish you can produce two copies per issue, one for your records and one for Mr Minte. I'm not suggesting that this is what you do; that would be dishonest, you see. I'm only pointing out one of the many possible moves in this game.

'Most importantly, Mr Minte didn't say what you should do with the rest of the money. So. You pay, say, two dollars a year for your newsletter and with the balance you can buy a typewriter and four filing cabinets every year for five years.

'You see, Mr Minte is very good and very generous; he's been playing international games for a long, long time and knows what's what. He wants you to have your typewriter and other things but won't say it. Go see him tomorrow and tell him that you'll do what he told you.

'But you must remember that in dealing with foreigners, never appear too smart; it's better that you look humble and half-primitive, especially while you're learning the ropes. And try to take off six stone. It's necessary that we're seen to be starved and needy. The reason why Tiko gets very little aid money is that our people are too fat and jolly. I wish the government would wake up and do something about it.'

And so, Emi Bagarap, whose self-respect had been shelved

for years, went on giving his friend, the novice, the benefit of his vast experience in the ways of the world.

When Ole left the office he was relieved and almost happy. He had begun to understand the complexities of life. Give me time, O Lord, he prayed as he headed toward the bus stop, and I'll be out there with the best of them.

'A word with you, old friend,' Manu's voice checked him.

'Oh, hello Manu. Long time no see. Where've you been?'

'Watching you lately, old friend. You have that look on your face,' Manu said simply.

'What look?' asked Ole in puzzlement.

'Of someone who's been convinced by the likes of Emi Bagarap. I'm worried about you. I know you and Emi have always been close, but allow me to tell you this before it's too late. Don't let him or anyone like him talk you into something you . . . .'

'No one talks me into anything. I've never allowed anyone to do that,' Ole cut in with visible irritation.

'You're already into it, old friend; it's written all over your face. Beware of Emi; he's sold his soul and will have you sell yours if you don't watch out.'

'That's ridiculous. No one's sold his soul. We're only shelving certain things for a little while until we get what's good for the country.'

'No, no, old friend. You're deceiving yourself. You're not shelving anything; you're set to sell your soul no less. Do it and you'll never get it back because you will not want to.'

'You're wasting your time and mine, Manu. You belong to the past; it's time to wake up to the future,' Ole snapped and strode away.

Next day when he met Mr Minte he was all smiles. The smoothly seasoned diplomat raised an eyebrow and smiled back—he was familiar with this kind of transformation; it happened all the time; it was part of his job to make it happen.

'Well, Ole, when will you form the committee?'

'Tonight, sir.'

'Congratulations, Mr Chairman. Get your secretary to write me a letter and you'll get your first $2000 in a month's time.'

'Thank you very, very much Mr Minte; I'm most grateful.'

'You're welcome. It's been a pleasure dealing with you, Ole. You have a big future ahead. If you need anything, anything at all, don't hesitate to contact me. You know, if we had more people like you around, the Pacific would develop so rapidly you wouldn't see it.'

They shook hands, and as Ole opened the door Mr Minte called out, 'By the way, the INESCA will soon hold a workshop in Manila on the proper methods of collecting oral traditions. It'll do you good if you attend. I'll let you know in a few weeks.'

'Thank you again, Mr Minte.'

'Don't mention it. I'm always happy to be of assistance. Goodbye for now. I hope you'll soon get a typewriter and the filing cabinets.'

Ole whistled his way home, much elated. That evening he formed the Committee for the Collection of Oral Traditions with himself as chairman and treasurer, his youngest brother as secretary, two friends as committee members, and the district officer as patron. The Committee immediately set to work drafting a letter to Mr Minte which was delivered by hand the following morning. Within a month Ole received a cheque for $2000 and an invitation to attend a six-week training course in Manila. He went, leaving his house in the care of his elderly aunt, who did not understand what he was doing.

He found the course too confusing, but the throbbing nightlife of Manila more than compensated for its uselessness. He enjoyed himself so much that on the third week he received a shot of penicillin and some friendly counsel from an understanding physician.

On his return journey he bought a duty-free typewriter in Sydney, where he also ordered four filing cabinets to be shipped home. He was much pleased with his speedy progress: he had secured what had only recently been a dream. One day, he told himself as the aircraft approached the Tikomalu International Airport, he would take over the directorship of the Bureau for the Preservation of Traditional Culture and Essential Indigenous Personality. Both Sailosi

Atiu and Eric Hobsworth-Smith were getting long in the tooth.

When he finally arrived home his aged aunt greeted him tearfully. 'Ole, Ole, you're safe. Thank God those heathens didn't eat you. You look so thin; what did they do to you?'

'Don't worry, auntie,' Ole laughed. 'Those people aren't heathens, they're mainly Catholics, and they don't eat people. They only shoot each other.'

'You look so sick. Did they try to shoot you too?'

'I'm perfectly healthy . . . except that I stubbed my big toe one night,' and he chortled.

'You should always wear shoes when you go overseas; I told you so, Ole. What's the matter? Why are you giggling?'

'The house looks so neat,' Ole deftly changed the subject. 'Thank you for looking after it; I know that I can always depend on you.'

'Oh, Ole, I cleared and scrubbed the whole place from top to bottom; it was in such a mess. You need a wife to clean up after you. Why don't you get married? Yes, Ole, you were always messy, leaving things all over the place. You haven't changed, really you haven't.' She paused to dry her face. 'I threw out so much rubbish,' she said in a tone that alarmed Ole.

'You did, did you? And what did you do with my books?'

'Books? What books?'

'Those exercise books I stacked at the corner back there.'

'You mean those used-up filthy things? Oh, Ole, you shouldn't have kept your old school books. They collected so much dust and so many cockroaches.'

'They're the most important things in my life. I cannot live without them,' he declared and went looking for his books.

'They aren't here. What have you done with them?' he demanded rather crossly.

'Sit down, Ole, and let's talk like good Christians.'

'No! Where are they?'

'Ole, you've always been a good boy. Sit down and have something to eat. You must be starving. What have they done to you?'

'Never mind that, I want my books!'

'Sit down and don't scream at me. That's a good boy. We're poor, you, me, the neighbours. And food is so expensive.'

'Where are my books?'

'Toilet paper is beyond our reach. It used to be ten cents a roll.'

'Yes, but what has that got to do with my books?'

'You didn't leave me any money when you went away, Ole. I had to eat and keep clean, and things are so expensive.'

'I'm sorry, but where are my books?'

'Don't keep asking me that question, Ole. I'm trying to explain. I'm your only living aunt. And I'm very old and ready to go to Heaven. Don't hasten me along, please. Don't you think that I'm more important than any old book?'

'What did you do with them? Where are they?'

'Ole, I had no money for food; I had no money for toilet paper. I had to eat and keep clean. Stop looking at me like that. You frighten me so.' She sniffed, blew her nose, then continued in a subdued tone. 'I used some and sold the rest cheaply to the neighbours. They're poor, Ole, but they also have to be hygienic.'

Ole stared at his aunt in disbelief. 'No, no. You're pulling my leg: you didn't really sell my books for toilet paper . . . .'

'I did. Yes, yes I did. I'm sorry but how could I have known they were so important?'

'Oh, my God!' Ole choked in anguish. He sat very still, breathing deeply, trying desperately to stop his arms from lashing out. Then slowly, very slowly, he mumbled, 'Seven years' hard work down the bloody drain; shit!' Almost immediately the import of what he had uttered sank in and he burst into hysterical laughter, with tears streaming down his cheeks. It was also then that the brilliant idea occurred to him. He reached out and embraced his aunt, apologising for his rudeness, promising never to do it again, and the old lady was so surprised at the transformation that she sobbed with tears of joy.

He recalled that he had Mr Minte's government committed

to $10 000 over five years. That was to be the start; he, Ole Pasifikiwei, whose books had gone down the drain, would henceforth go after the whales of the ocean. If he were to beg, he informed himself, he might as well do it on the grand scale. He therefore sent Mr Minte an urgent letter and was soon rewarded with the arrival of Dr Andrew Wheeler, a razor-sharp expert upon whose advice Ole instituted the National Council for Social, Economic, and Cultural Research, bagging chiefs, ministers of state, top-flight clergymen, wives of VIPs, and his old friend, Emi Bagarap, into honorary office-holding positions, with himself as full-time secretary. Then Dr Wheeler devised a comprehensive four-year research program and despatched professionally-worded letters to the INESCA, the Forge Foundation, the Friends of South Sea Natives, the Third World Conservation Commission, and the Konshu Fish and Forestry Institute for $400 000 funding.

A little later, and again with the skilled connivance of his indispensable Dr Wheeler, Ole expanded by creating eighteen other national committees and councils with specific, aid-worthy objectives, and designed irresistibly attractive projects and schemes to be funded from international sources. And he capped it all by succeeding in getting his groups placed by the Great International Organisation on the list of the Two Hundred Least Developed Committees—those in need of urgent, generous aid.

After six years Ole had applied for a total of $14 million for his organisations, and his name had become well known in certain influential circles in Brussels, The Hague, Bonn, Geneva, Paris, London, New York, Washington, Wellington, Canberra, Tokyo, Peking, and Moscow, as well as in such regional laundry centres as Bangkok, Kuala Lumpur, Manila, Suva, and Noumea.

And the University of the Southern Paradise, whose wise, wily leaders saw in the man a great kindred talent that matched their own, bestowed upon him honorary doctoral degrees in Economics, Divinity, and Philosophy, although that learned institution had no philosophy of any kind, colour, or creed.

With fame and honour to his name, Ole Pasifikiwei immersed himself totally in the supreme task of development through foreign aid, relishing the twists and turns of international funding games. He has since shelved his original sense of self-respect and has assumed another, more attuned to his new, permanent role as a first-rate, expert beggar.

More about Penguins

For further information about books available from Penguin please write to the following:

In New Zealand: For a complete list of books available from Penguin in New Zealand write to the Marketing Department, Penguin Books (N.Z.) Ltd, Private Bag, Takapuna, Auckland.

In Australia: For a complete list of books available from Penguin in Australia write to the Marketing Department, Penguin Books Australia Ltd, P.O. Box 257, Ringwood, Victoria 3134.

In Britain: For a complete list of books available from Penguin in Britain write to Dept EP, Penguin Books Ltd, Harmondsworth, Middlesex UB7 0DA.

In the U.S.A.: For a complete list of books available from Penguin in the United States write to Dept DG, Penguin Books, 299 Murray Hill Parkway, East Rutherford, New Jersey 07073.

In Canada: For a complete list of books available from Penguin in Canada write to Penguin Books Canada Ltd, 2801 John Street, Markham, Ontario L3R 1B4.